Stirling Conspiracy

Anne-Marie Price

This novel is entirely a work of fiction.
The names, characters and incidents portrayed in it
are the work of the Author's imagination.
Any resemblance to actual persons, living or dead,
events or localities is entirely coincidental

ISBN: 978-0-9942761-4-8

DEDICATION

To Shirley and Len Daley,
who encouraged me
to believe in my dreams.

The Stirling Breed Trilogy

2016
Stirling Breed
Stirling Masquerade
Stirling Conspiracy

ACKNOWLEDGMENTS

Stella Eversden
A gem of a Proof Reader.

Helen Iles
For convincing me to split
Stirling Breed into three novels.

Rebecca Schulz
For her invaluable information
in regards to beards

Trilogy Review

Stirling Breed

Brought up more a boy than a girl, Lady Antonia (Tony) Stirling had been determinedly resisting the pressure to act like a woman and marry until she met Lord Caleb Delacourt. Now their love threatens the future prospects of at least five people. When an abduction attempt of Tony and her much younger brother, Lord Aidan was thwarted by Caleb, a more daring plan is undertaken. A second abduction is attempted, and when Caleb comes to their rescue again, he is blinded. The trio are transported from England to France. With the very recent defeat of Napoleon at Waterloo, France is a very hostile environment to be trapped within. Even though they manage to escape their abductor, fleeing the country will not be as easy.

Stirling Masquerade

In desperate need for help, the trio must pretend to be a French family as they make their way to Paris and possible aid to get them home. Leaving Paris becomes complicated as Aidan falls ill and those possibly behind their abduction arrive in Paris to look for the escapees. Although it is hard to know who they can trust, the masqueraders are not completely friendless in such a hostile land. With their enemies closing in on them, they are forced to risk Aidan's health and attempt to evade capture as they head for the coast. With freedom so close, they are ambushed and although Caleb suffers further injuries, the friends they had made in Paris assist the masqueraders in their desire to just go home.

TUESDAY
I'd Rather Let Them Sleep

When the yacht silently docked back into Birling Gap, off the Sussex coast, Louise and the Earl looked in on the masqueraders and they were all peacefully asleep. Nothing startling, untoward or remotely frightening had occurred on the journey across the Channel; they had slept the whole way. His expression softening as he watched the contented scene, the Earl decided to not wake them just yet. His Lordship's carriage had been stabled at the Anchor Inn and as the horses were being harnessed, the luggage loaded on the roof of the carriage, the Earl was considering their options.

Gathering his companions but not disturbing the masqueraders, the Earl put to them his suggestion.

'I want to let them sleep for a little longer so I'd like to send half of us on ahead to the Manor where they can then be making sure that everything is prepared while the carriage returns for the other half. Or the Innkeeper has offered to hire out his carriage and we all travel home in convoy.'

The others looked at each other but it was Andre who spoke, 'I understand why you don't want to disturb Caleb; his pain will be overwhelming but I'd prefer it if we went together. I'd rather be close at hand as those children really don't have the energy to cope with anything else.' The rest of the group as one nodded in agreement.

'Well then,' accepted the Earl, 'Patrick, you'd better arrange with Charlie the Innkeeper, the hire of his carriage. Geoff, I've left orders for the yacht crew to carry Claude's body to Doctor

Stevenson's surgery; can you just organise the coffin and cart needed to transport it up to London? Andre, can you consider how best to seat all of us? Unfortunately we'll have to take Nigel Sutherland with us until we can be relieved of his presence by the Bow Street Runners. Louise, if you could come with me to wake up my children. Caleb may still have an itchy trigger finger and could be disorientated when first woken.'

Accepting their orders, they dispersed and even though it was still dark outside, the day was promising to be fair and cloud free.

More Unbelievable Pain

Earl Stirling had been right to be worried about Caleb's reaction to being woken but the moment the door opened, Tony sat up and silently gestured for her father and Louise to enter but not to speak.

'Caleb? Caleb, Papa has brought us back to England. We need to get up now.' Tony spoke softly and gently, nodding as Louise picked up the medical bag. The Earl reached over Tony to pick up Aidan to bundle him up into his blankets again but Caleb's arm snapped like steel round the boy. The Earl backed off until Tony managed to wake her fiancé.

'Caleb, it's time to go home.' She placed a tender kiss against his lips but as she felt him waken, she slid her hand over Aidan's ears. Unrestrained colourful language issued, as Caleb's return to consciousness also meant he was in incredible pain. Louise found in the medical bag the sachets Doctor Girard had provided for pain relief and even before he managed to sit up, she placed a couple of sachets into a glass of water and handed him the glass.

'We'll be leaving as soon as you can get up.' The Earl spoke softly as he was certain that his future son-in-law had a headache that would stun an elephant. He left Louise to assist them to get ready as Caleb drank his medicine in one go.

For a moment Caleb slumped back against his pillow but now that he was finally sentient allowed Louise to pick up Aidan and rewrap him back into his blankets for the journey. Tony slipped out of the bed, stretching before putting her boots back on. She looked fondly at the bag she had used as her baby bump but apart from removing any remaining money, documents and her jewellery to place into her jacket pockets, Tony gladly discarded it.

The yacht crew took out their luggage to be loaded with the rest, but Caleb insisted on keeping his boots, a clean jacket and his weapons. Louise assisted him to dress but left the cabin until it was time to depart.

Awake, sort of, dressed and rearmed, Caleb had slumped for a moment as he sat upon the bed. Tony and Aidan remained silent in respect for his headache except when one of the yacht crew, having removed their luggage, offered Tony a bar of chocolate for Aidan. She thanked him but when he tried to pick up the medical bag Tony shook her head. The crew member bowed respectfully and left the room.

Breaking off a small piece of chocolate, she placed it into her brother's mouth as his hands were wrapped underneath the blankets again, Aidan sucked quietly on the chocolate enthusiastically until it had dissolved completely.

'Papa?'

'Yes Little Bear?' Caleb answered automatically.

'Is your head very bad?'

Caleb managed a tired smile. 'It feels like someone is using it to play the drums.'

'Would you like some chocolate?'

Caleb was touched by the offer as he knew that the five year old adored his chocolate. 'Thank you but no, although if another couple of sachets of pain relief are on offer, I'd be grateful.'

Tony refrained from comment as she placed another couple of sachets into a glass of water before handing it to him. *I'm not sure how many sachets Caleb can take before it becomes dangerous. Doctor Girard had told me 'two every four or six hours' but Doctor Masters will probably examine us as soon as we arrive home and will advise me as to correct dosage.*

Allowing Tony to take the glass out of his hand again, Caleb finally sat up a little straighter and stretched some of his aching joints and muscles.

'You know Aidan,' he said gently, 'now that we're back in England you may speak in English again and for the sake of your parents, you no longer need to call Tony and myself 'Mama and Papa.' It really had a nice sound to it Little Bear and your father took it rather manfully when you called him Grandpapa in Paris but I don't think Charlotte will be able to handle you calling anyone else Mama, especially not Tony.'

There was a moment of silence as the small boy processed all this information. 'Are we safe then?'

Caleb sighed. *I am not going to lie to my future brother.* 'I don't know, not yet. Safe enough that we no longer have to pretend to be the French Rene, Bella and Henri Du Bois. As for any additional dangers here in England, I just don't know.' Turning slightly on the bed, Caleb's hand searched until he found the heavily wrapped Aidan and drew him into a hug.

'But I promise you that whatever we must face next, you will always be safe with us,' he added. Unable to get his arms free to wrap around Caleb's neck, Aidan laid his head onto Caleb's undamaged shoulder and Tony, with tears in her eyes, allowed them to sit like that for a couple of minutes.

It Is Unbelievable!

Bending to pick up Aidan, Tony said softly, 'Time to go home boys.' She gathered up the medical bag before laying her hand on Caleb's shoulder. She was about to help him to his feet when the cabin door burst open. All of a sudden, gone was his tiredness, gone was his pain as Caleb reached out with one hand to grasp Tony's and dragged her and Aidan behind him while his other hand withdrew a pistol and pointed it directly at the intruder. The only thing that stopped him from actually pulling the trigger was Tony's voice.

'Stop Caleb. It's Doctor Stevenson,' she explained, a little surprised by the Doctor's appearance as it seemed that he had merely pulled an overcoat over his nightwear. He still had slippers on his feet and was quite out of breath as he had run all the way from his home.

'Caleb, I don't think you've officially met the Doctor as you were unconscious when he attended to your burns.' Tony laid her hand over Caleb's and gently persuaded him to lower his weapon.

'My apologises, Lord Delacourt, I should've realised that you'd still be in warrior mode but when your cousin said you were back safe in England, I wanted to check on how your injuries have healed.' Doctor Stevenson gasped for breath, *it has been a long time since I had to run anywhere or any distance.*

After a brief moment, Caleb holstered his pistol. 'Thank you but Tony re-bandaged my wounds after cleaning up the new hole in my head.'

Easing Caleb down onto the edge of the bed, the Doctor looked over the bandages in professional interest. 'Well it has stopped the bleeding for now so I'll leave it for your local Doctor to examine when he manages to get a good look at all three of you.' The Doctor had cupped Caleb's chin between his hands as he raised his face and Caleb drew back.

'Please don't kiss me!'

Removing his hands, the Doctor blinked twice before glancing across at Tony who smiled in sympathy of his confusion.

'Sorry Doctor Stevenson but the French are a little too enthusiastic with their kissing. It was a trial for his Lordship.'

Relieved Doctor Stevenson smiled. 'Oh I see. Actually I was just admiring your beard, my Lord, as it really does make you look like a different man from the one I treated less than a week ago.' Turning to face Tony he peeked under the fur hood of the coat that enveloped Aidan. 'Peek a boo! How are you little man? Have you been taking care of these young lovers?' The Doctor noted the extensive blanket system under the fur coat and pressed his hand against the boy's forehead.

'Mama... Tony took care of both of us.' Aidan said, 'I became sick.' He sighed deeply as if everything was all his fault.

'Little Bear, we've discussed this,' Caleb's tone was soft but also a little stern. 'You didn't want to become sick did you?'

'No,' Aidan meekly agreed. 'But...'

Doctor Stevenson gently patted the boy's cheek. You have a compromised immune system young man. All that has befallen all of you is because Nigel Sutherland stole you once again from your home. Do you understand me?' Carefully he wiped away the tear that fell down Aidan's cheek.

'Yes Sir,' sighing deeply, Aidan raised his eyes to his sister's. 'Can we please go home now?'

Tony smiled. 'Yes Little Bear, we're going home.' She extended the arm not holding her brother to place under Caleb's elbow to help him to his feet again.

Following the young family up on deck, Doctor Stevenson assisted Caleb over the side of the yacht, since Tony had her hands full with Aidan, before pausing to exchange greetings with the Earl. Having heard the news of the abductees' return, the Doctor had not stopped to speak to anyone on the dock or heed Andre's warning before he boarded the boat.

Earl Stirling expressed his mild surprise that Doctor Stevenson still had his head firmly attached to his body as Andre assisted Caleb, Tony and Aidan into the Earl's carriage. In the second carriage Rosemary, Louise and François were already inside, with each of the two women calmly pointing a pistol towards Nigel who sat, hands bound, opposite them. Andre would be joining the second carriage as Patrick and Geoff would travel with the Earl.

Andre decided the best thing to do was keep Nigel as far away from Caleb as possible. *One wrong word from that man could easily result in him sharing Claude's fate. Even so I am not happy about Rosemary's continued uneasiness regarding Geoff and Patrick but if Nigel is in collusion with either cousin or both, it would be unwise to have all of them in the same vehicle.*

Just before they set off, Andre pressed a spare pistol into Tony's hand and was relieved when she didn't reject it but placed it into the pocket of her overcoat before settling Aidan on her lap so that he might sleep all the way home.

Chasing The Dawn

Once again, two carriages swept through the silent and dark countryside, this time of Sussex. It was after all still only about one o'clock in the morning. It was, though, Tony hoped, the final leg of their adventure. She could feel Caleb sitting very upright beside her, stiff as a board in an attempt to stay awake, alert, and ready for any more trouble if it came. When Tony suggested to him that he should lean his head against her shoulder and try to sleep, he shook his head. He allowed some of the stiffness to seep out of his body as he tried to relax and drawing Tony closer to him, placed his arm around her waist.

Leaning her head against Caleb's shoulder, Tony wondered, *Is Papa trying to decide how to tell Charlotte that her brother has been involved with the abduction of her son and their future son-in-law has been forced to kill Claude to protect us? Worse perhaps will be that same conversation with Agnes Henry.* A frown descended upon Tony's brow as she contemplated, *have I underestimated Claude's intelligence if, and it is a big if, he were the master mind behind the second abduction and the plan to kill us all.*

These musings were cut short when they heard a shot fired close to the driver and a shouted order of 'Stand and deliver!' The carriages drew to a stop as Caleb removed his arm from around Tony's waist and drew both his pistols from his holsters. Tony was still frowning in concentration but for a different reason this time.

'Did the Highwayman's voice sound familiar to you?' Tony asked, tightening her arms around Aidan.

'Solitaire?' suggested the Earl.

Caleb shook his head, then wished he hadn't done that as it made his head hurt even more. 'Almost but... not quite right.'

As the truth suddenly hit her, Tony laughed and when the carriage door was opened from the outside, she spoke to the Highwayman.

'Good morning Gerry. Haven't you spoken to your brother Albert? You're out of the Highwayman business.'

The bandit's ready spiel dried up in surprise and he lowered the muffler that covered the lower half of his face. 'Lady Tony? You're safe! Aye Al told us the good fortune but while he's working with Lord Stirling's people to do up the farm, we still need to put food on the table.' Gerry gestured to include the four armed horsemen that surrounded both carriages.

The Earl drew out his purse and selected a few notes. 'Take this Gerry and go home for tonight. In the morning you and the rest of your family can report to my Farm Manager.'

Although Gerry took the money, he protested, 'We don't want charity my Lord.'

'You'll be paid like any other employee and you'll need help teaching those boys of yours how to run the farm once it's up and running again.'

'Papa,' Aidan had been woken by the gun shot and voices. 'Their sheep need shearing.'

'There you go Gerry, your first job already lined up.' The Earl was pleased with his son. *Not only has Aidan come up with a useful suggestion but also he did not wake up screaming or crying from the gun shot.* What Lord Stirling didn't realise was that after what they had been through over the last week or more, Aidan truly believed it when Caleb had told him that he would always be safe with Caleb and Tony.

'Thank you, my Lord.' Gerry bowed, 'as the boys and I are heading your way, we'll escort you home. We wouldn't want you to fall into the hands of unscrupulous Highwaymen now would we?' With a chuckle, Gerry shut the carriage door and signalled to one of his sons who brought his horse over for Gerry to mount. So not for the first time Tony and Caleb were escorted back to the Manor by a Highwayman.

Home At Last!

The Stirling Manor was sent into a flurry of noise and activity upon the arrival of the two vehicles. Grooms unloading luggage, Maids making up extra beds for the visitors, Cook putting on the kettle for hot drinks all round and Mary, extracting Caleb, Tony and Aidan from the chaos, led them upstairs to Caleb's bedroom. She sat them down in peace and quiet as she lit the fire. The Earl had been eager to send for Doctor Masters immediately but as Caleb's head had not started bleeding again, Tony insisted they called the Doctor after they'd all had some sleep.

Charlotte wept at the sight of her family returned safely home and Andre quietly suggested to the Earl that news of her brother's demise should be left until the Countess had recovered a little. The Earl, who was uncomfortable around tears and excessive emotions, was grateful to accept the Author's advice. So Lizzy was directed to take Charlotte back to her bed and the removal of so much emotion caused more than one traveller to sigh in relief.

The French contingent of the travellers were a little uneasy at first as to their place in the Stirling household. Here they weren't servants but they weren't aristocracy either. Rosemary was more conscious of this limbo and clung to Andre's hand as they were led into the parlour where a dressing gown attired Frederick and Patience Sinclair, Lady Margarette and Duncan Gray were introduced. Before Mary had dragged her away to solitude, Tony had a quiet word with Mrs Preston so that the Housekeeper understood that their French guests were to be placed into guest rooms and not the servants' quarters. Tony didn't want anyone to feel uncomfortable so she wanted this clear from the start.

The Earl was a little disappointed that Tony had disappeared with Caleb and Aidan upstairs instead of joining her grandparents in the parlour. The Dowager Countess, though, was more impressed that her granddaughter was diligent in her duties to her patients and told her son that there was plenty of time for reunions after they had breakfast.

Even so, Tony left Mary in charge of the fire to warm Aidan while Lady Isabella sat with her son so that Tony could greet her own relatives. No one asked for any details of their adventure as she would tell them when she was ready. As soon as Tony began to become a little edgy about being away from Caleb's and Aidan's side, Lady Margarette sent everyone off to bed.

A little nervous about walking through the corridors on her own, Tony didn't refuse the Footman, William's offer to escort her to Caleb's room. *I haven't worked out how we're going to handle the sleeping arrangements as I want both Caleb and Aidan to remain in the same room as me.* Knocking on the bedroom door and announcing her return, Tony entered to find that this problem has been taken care of. One folding bed had been set up in front of the fire place, Aidan had been dressed into a night shirt but as a precaution wore a think woollen jumper as he sat on his bed sipping his hot chocolate. Aidan looked up and smiled at his sister's return before returning to his absorption of chocolate.

An embarrassed Caleb had permitted Mary and his mother to also change his clothes ready for bed. Having read through Doctor Girard's instructions regarding Caleb's medication, Isabella decided that he could have two more cachets now but no more until dawn. Caleb had decided to join Aidan with hot chocolate, but he sat in one of the arm chairs rather than in bed.

Neither woman had managed to make him part with his pistols. Gesturing for Isabella to sit in the other arm chair, Tony took her mug from Mary and accepted Caleb's out-stretched hand to draw her onto his lap. To his mother's surprise, some of the anxiety that had increased in Caleb when Tony had left the room, now seemed to slide away from him. Tony smiled at Isabella in understanding.

'It's been... a very stressful time Lady Isabella and we're not absolutely certain that it's all over just yet.' She explained.

'What has become of that walking mountain you brought home with you?' Isabella accepted a cup of tea as she sat down opposite the young couple.

'I don't know. John Smythe, our Head Groom, will have locked him away for tonight or perhaps one of the Grooms will have delivered him to Squire Perkins, the local Justice of the Peace. Now that we're home, I suppose Papa will be in contact with London and we should expect to see a Bow Street Runner on our doorstep later today or tomorrow.'

Glancing around the room, Tony noticed that a second trundle bed had been set up on the other side of the room. 'Is that bed for me Mary?' she asked.

From her seat under the window, holding her own hot drink, Mary shook her head. 'No my Lady. I'll be sleeping in this rooms with you and William has volunteered to sit outside the door with a shot gun.'

Glancing furtively between Maid and mistress, Isabella asked, 'Where will Tony be sleeping?'

Mary looked a little startled as she thought that was obvious. 'Beside Lord Delacourt of course, my Lady.'

That caused his mother to raise a protest. 'Oh! No really! That is not at all appropriate!'

Mary smiled as she understood that it went against every rule set out for their class by society. 'Lady Delacourt, Lady Tony has more than likely spent the last five nights in his Lordship's bed. Although he has assured me, even though I didn't need it, that he was a gentleman during that time, it is imperative that the three of them remain together until they have recovered. If you can suggest a better way to organise their sleeping arrangements, I'm happy to comply, but I'm hoping that his Lordship will not wake up screaming in terror if Lady Tony is not there beside him.'

For a moment there was silence as Isabella tried to visualise how to overcome her reservations but had to concede that there was no other way.

Tony reached out and laid her hand over her future mother-in-law's. 'Caleb has told me that he wants his eyesight returned before we become intimate and by that time we'll be married anyway.'

'Oh! So there won't be any lengthy engagement?' Isabella was surprised at how fast they were intending to proceed.

After Doctor Masters has examined Caleb's burns and determined when he may take the dressings off completely, then no more than a couple of days after that. Doctor Masters will also prove there is no reason for a hasty wedding but we don't want to wait to start the rest of our lives together.'

Still a little doubtful, Isabella said, 'Caleb? Is that what you want?'

His head had fallen slightly forward onto his chest and Tony had removed the half empty cup from his fingers but upon being directly addressed he raised his head.

'Sorry Mama, did you want something? I'm so tired and in pain, that I just want to go to bed. To be honest I don't think I could sleep if Tony wasn't beside me. I'd be worrying if she was safe.' His words weren't exactly slurred but they were faint and Tony immediately rose from his lap and handing Mary the cups, she helped Caleb to his feet and across to the main bed.

Even without him having to ask, Tony returned for his pistols and placed one under his pillow and the other within easy reach. Mary collected up the other crockery and placed it all on a tray as Tony first tucked Aidan and then Caleb up in their beds.

'Tony,' Aidan whispered. 'Can I join you and Caleb if I get scared?' On seeing how brave the little boy was trying to be, all of Isabella's reservations vanished.

'Of course Little Bear, or if you get cold. Did you want to stay with us now, or do you prefer the heat of the fire?' Tony came back to sit on the bed beside her brother.

'Caleb?' Aidan was hesitant to disturb him. An understanding smile eased onto Caleb's face and he patted the bed beside him.

'Come one Little Bear, its way past all our bed times.' Caleb offered and in seconds Aidan scampered out of his bed and slid under the covers beside Caleb.

Tony placed Aidan's fur rug over the top of her brother before she allowed Mary to help her to change into a nightgown. Sitting on the edge of the main bed as Mary quickly brushed and plaited her hair, Tony raised questioning eyes to Isabella. The older woman had been swept away by this picture of family unity, a promise of their future together.

'I'll take Aidan's bed if you still are worried Lady Isabella.'

Suddenly understanding, Isabella shook her head. 'No, I have no further objections to your sleeping arrangements.' She came across to the bed, kissed her son on the cheek, Aidan on the top of his head as he was buried under his fur rug and moved around the bed to kiss Tony's cheek before tucking her into her son's bed.

Mary escorted a stunned Isabella to the door and curtsied as she let her out. The Maid gestured to William to see Lady Isabella to her bedroom before he settled down to watch over the occupants' well deserved slumber.

Inside the room, Mary hesitated over extinguishing any of the candles. Glancing down at her brother's curly mop of hair that poked out the top of his blanket, Tony made the decision for her Maid.

'Leave a candle or two burning for a little while, Mary. If you fall asleep before me, I'll extinguish them.'

Mary bent over to tenderly kiss her mistress' cheek. 'I think I'll sit up for a while. Sleep now my Lady, you've earned it.' Wrapping her dressing gown tighter around her nightgown, Mary sat down in one of the arm chairs and placing her knitting bag beside her feet, she too kept vigil.

A New Day

It is such a nice sensation. Waking up in the arms of the man I love. Feeling safe, content and at peace. Before she opened her eyes, Tony's other senses were assessing their current situation. *Something isn't quite right. My head is against Caleb's chest, his arms protectively wrapped around me but there should be something or more importantly someone between us.* Tony's body instantly stiffened as she realised what her senses had been trying to tell her. Aidan was no longer between the two adults. Her eyes flew open, a startled cry left her lips and she would have sprung from the bed but Caleb's strong arms kept her lying beside him.

'Calm down Tony, Aidan got up about an hour ago and is sitting with Mary,' Caleb's calm tone relieved her fear and he eased his hold on her so that she could sit up and see for herself. With a sigh of relief Tony sank back into her fiancé's arms and caressed her hand against his chest.

'Have you been awake since then? You should have woken me.' She leant up on one elbow so that she could kiss Caleb on the lips.

'Mary gave me some medication and I dozed for a while until it started to work. Time to get up elfling?'

With a sigh, she reluctantly agreed and drew herself out of Caleb's embrace. 'As much as I'd rather stay in bed with you, I suppose there are a number of things we need to do today.' As Tony stretched, Mary rose to her feet and placed Aidan into the chair she had just vacated.

'What first my Lady? Breakfast or a bath?'

Sitting up Caleb threw back the bed covers. 'Something a little more urgent,' he said.

Giggling, Aidan jumped off the chair and went over to the bed to take Caleb's hand. 'I need to pee, Papa... Caleb.'

Smiling Caleb reached out his other hand to caress the boy's cheek. 'It'll take time getting used to your old life again,' he reassured and allowed the boy to help him to his feet.

'Then breakfast?' asked Tony, actually feeling hungry for a change.

'Yes,' Caleb agreed, half way out the door before he was even allowed to put on a dressing gown. William, still on duty, escorted them down to the bathroom while Mary straightened the bed and Tony pulled the bell to order breakfast.

Doctor Masters' Examination

They ate, bathed and dressed. Tony had washed her hair as well as Aidan's and was relieved that the black dye had come out immediately. Both siblings were ordered to sit in front of the fire to dry their hair before Mary would allow them to do anything else.

So it was to this cosy domestic scene that Doctor Stanley Masters was escorted to examine the masqueraders. Even though Charles, the Footman, had announced the Doctor's arrival, they saw the glint of steel as Caleb still kept his pistols close at hand. William was sent off to bed, having been on guard duty since they had arrived at the Manor. Mary would also retire once she had assisted the Doctor with his examinations, especially of Tony.

Doctor Masters recommended that Aidan remain in bed for two more days but could return to a normal diet. It was important to keep him warm, free from drafts and away from any possible chance of relapse or infection. That meant that anyone who had so much as a sniffle was sent away from the Manor until they were well again.

The Doctor was pleased to report that the only evidence of Tony's adventure seemed to be a healing sprained wrist and bruises around her throat from Claude holding her in front of him as a shield before Caleb killed him. Although it was embarrassing, Tony endured in silence yet another virginity check and was relieved when Doctor Masters gave his seal of approval.

As Mary was allowed to re-dress Tony into one of Charlotte's altered dresses, the Doctor did voice his surprise. When Caleb coloured up, Doctor Masters hastened to reassure him.

'I'm not casting doubt upon your honour, my Lord. I just would have understood if you had given in to your desires. I mean you had no way of knowing if you were going to survive this adventure.'

Smiling, Tony shook her head. 'I never doubted that Caleb would get us home safely. We were offered more than once the opportunity to be married in France but Caleb wanted to wait and do it properly.'

There was a momentary silence as Doctor Masters sat Caleb down on the edge of the bed and began to unwind his bandages. 'Really? Sorry, I'm not doubting your noblesse oblige but I would've wanted some tender loving to make me forget the nightmare I was living. Especially in the compete darkness.'

'We had our moments of stress relief,' Caleb admitted. 'The important factor though was that Aidan was with us the whole time.'

'As he is now gentlemen,' there was more than a little note of warning in Tony's voice, 'so please change the subject!'

Embarrassed at forgetting his manners, Doctor Masters concentrated on examining Caleb's burns and then the bullet graze.

'You've done an excellent job keeping the burns clean and sterile. Especially as I believe you've not been bandaging the whole area during the day.'

'We were trying to be less conspicuous,' Tony explained, taking Caleb's hand as he manfully tolerated the Doctor's examination.

'Understood. Just not ideal. Well you were lucky with this bullet wound my Lord. A fraction to the left and you wouldn't be here right now.' Placing a fresh dressing over the bullet graze, Doctor Masters took Tony's free hand to hold it in place while he examined Caleb's closed eyes.

From his medical bag, the Doctor brought out a small bottle which the lid, when unscrewed, contained its own dropper. 'Keep your eyes closed my Lord, while I add a couple of drops. Then when I tell you, slowly open your eyes.'

Caleb's voice was a little faint when he spoke, 'I thought it'd be a couple more days before we could test my sight?'

'Hum, I'd hazard a guess that at the moment of the explosion you instinctively closed your eyes. In that case all the damage should be external. You'll probably have to reapply the ointment more regularly once the bandages come off your eyes as blinking and excessive eye movement will increase your discomfort.' Doctor Masters placed a couple of drops into each of Caleb's eyes and gestured to Mary. 'Close the curtains please, direct sunlight should be avoided until the burns have healed.'

As the natural light was shut out of the room, Doctor Masters lit a candle on the bedside table. Tony tried to breathe normally but her ribs had tightened remorselessly around her lungs.

'Open your eyes, my Lord, don't panic if everything is a little blurry.' The Doctor stood back so that he could watch Caleb's reactions as he cautiously opened his eyes. He suppressed the instinct to rub his hand across his eyes as that would hurt the burnt eyelids like hell. Caleb blinked a couple of times and allowed his vision time to adjust to the muted light before he finally raised his eyes to meet Tony's worried face. A slow smile spread across his face.

'My elfling, you're more beautiful than I remember you to be! Although you do seem to be a little out of focus.' Caleb's words brought a sob to Tony's throat and a tear of relief fell down her cheek. 'My love, don't cry.' He reached up one, not quite steady, hand to brush away her tears as Doctor Masters picked up the candle beside the bed and moved it in front of Caleb's face. Satisfied by the reactions of the pupils, Doctor Masters blew out the candle.

'The blurriness should ease in time so long as you don't do anything foolish in the next five days.'

Caleb grinned. 'You mean like being abducted and transported to a foreign country?'

Patting Caleb's shoulder indulgently, the Doctor agreed. 'Yes, exactly! At night bandage and anoint as you have been. During the day, until the bullet wound has healed, dress the graze. I'll try and find some dark lens instead of the black lens of your glasses for day use.' Masters placed a dressing over the forehead burns and the bullet graze before securing it with a bandage.

When the Doctor had packed up his bag, a small voice came from beside the fireplace. 'Caleb?'

He looked up and smiled at the worried little boy. 'Yes Little Bear? Oh, you've found Bunny again!'

Uttering a gurgle of laughter, Aidan launched himself off the trundle bed and into Caleb's arms. Soothingly Caleb brushed his hand down the boy's hair.

'It's all right little brother,' he reached up to take Tony's hand into his own and found that hers was trembling. 'We're all going to be all right.' Drawing her down to sit on the bed beside him, Caleb released Tony's hand to cup her face and sought her lips beneath his. Sobbing in relief, Tony at first shyly, then more passionately met his kiss. Mary smiled indulgently but Doctor Masters tut-tutted.

'Enough of that children, you're not married yet!'

The embracing couple broke off in embarrassment but Aidan looking up at them, cast a look of scorn at the Doctor as Mary opened the bedroom door for his departure.

'They're only kissing!' said Aidan, dismissively. 'They're allowed to do that now.'

The Doctor chuckled, 'Maybe so Lord Aidan, but I know where kissing can lead hot and passionate young lovers! I'll check on you tomorrow unless you run into any complications.' He bowed before heading downstairs to let Earl Stirling and Lady Isabella know how their children fared.

A House Within A House

As their relatives downstairs rejoiced at the news, Tony considered the various ways she could keep her boys entertained as they would be confined to the bedroom until the Doctor declared it was safe for Aidan to leave. Before Mary was sent off to her own bed, she brought up that morning's newspapers, several books from the library, but as Caleb requested, nothing in French and no melodramas. Duncan tried to encourage Aidan to do a little school work but only managed to leave some books the boy was prepared to read with his sister.

Visitors were permitted so long as they passed the health requirements but they were not encouraged by Doctor's orders to stay long. The stress they had been under throughout their trek through France meant that the masqueraders needed time and quiet to let their nerves settle back into normal life.

Earl Stirling left for London to inform his mother-in-law of Claude's death and deliver Nigel Sutherland to the appropriate Authorities. Charlotte and Lizzy had handled quite well the news that their brother was dead. That was until Lizzy wondered, *if mother is somehow going to lay the blame of Claude's death at our door?* The Earl promised that he wouldn't let their mother upset them but the sisters were still in doubt until Lady Margarette rather bluntly stated that since neither sister was actually in France she couldn't possibly see how they could be held accountable for their brother's crimes, activities or even his death.

The Earl took Patrick to London. In part to keep an eye on Nigel Sutherland on the journey but also to find out what stories were already circulating the metropolis about the flight through France. They still didn't know if Claude had been the instigator of the abduction or if he had just been following orders and who had been keeping the London Press up to date on the masqueraders' plight.

The Earl believed in his nephew's motives, Caleb had been reassured in his trust of his cousin Geoff, but Tony still had doubts about who she could really trust. She didn't share her fears with anyone, afraid that they'd say she was being paranoid or over-sensitive. When Tony noticed that Caleb's hand still automatically went for his pistols whenever there was a knock at the door, she felt less foolish about her own fears.

As they were unable to leave Caleb's room, Charlotte was perhaps justified when she stated that although the masqueraders were home, they weren't really home. Caleb's room had become a separate house and although the other members of the Manor were allowed to visit, they were not free to come and go as they pleased.

Tony thought, *it is strange that Charlotte seems to be interested in her child now that access is restricted*, but she kept that to herself, not wishing to upset or alienate her step-mother. Tony tried to suppress the uncharitable thought, *Charlotte is jealous of my close relationship with my half-brother and sees he clearly prefers my company*, or the more scandalous idea that, *Charlotte is upset at how close she came to losing the heir to the Stirling title, especially if Claude had been behind the abduction.*

Tony Shows Off Her Pregnant Look

Allowing the fire to die out, Tony had carefully opened the curtains, being sure that Caleb was not affected by the light and opened a window to allow some fresh air into the room. Aidan, draped in his fur rug, made certain that he didn't get too cool. Before Mary had retired to sleep, she had taken the carpet bag of dirty clothing down to the laundry area and put Caleb's blood-stained attire into a trough of soapy water to soak.

Rosemary, not sure what to do with herself, sorted out Tony's and Caleb's clean clothes from the other carpet bag and separated out the borrowed attire that would be returned to their original owners. She very carefully hung up Tony's wedding dress and put aside the material for the doll-maker Bridget. Before Rosemary could unpack the baby bump bag, Tony briefly slipped it on under one of Louise's borrowed dresses so that her female relatives but more importantly Caleb could see her pretend pregnancy.

Understanding that Caleb would not be able to handle a large invasion of women into his room, Tony left him in charge of Aidan and took Charlotte, Lizzy, Lady Margarette, Isabella and Patience Sinclair to her room. They marvelled over Tony's choice for a wedding dress which was very unusual by the day's fashions but Lady Margarette stated calmly that ivory was a much better choice for a young lady of Tony's colouring than white or pink.

Rosemary assisted Tony to change into one of Louise's dresses and the baby bump. The result was a stunned silence from the other ladies as Tony blushed becomingly at being stared at so intently. Charlotte wondered vaguely, *had it been my mother's accursed diet that made my own pregnancy with Aidan look more like a deformity, all skin and bones and a bulging belly? Whereas Tony looks natural and even glowing.* Uttering a half sob Charlotte threw her arms around a surprised Tony's neck.

'Oh dear Tony, you're going to make a beautiful bride and a very natural mother!' Charlotte kissed her step-daughter's cheek and quickly left the room before her emotions got the better of her. In surprise Tony raised questioning eyes to each of her grandmothers. Patience ran a gentle hand down Tony's hair.

'You accept this look with grace and dignity my darling girl, just like your mother did,' said Patience, 'Charlotte didn't like being pregnant which could be why Aidan doesn't have any younger brothers or sisters until now.'

'Oh! I didn't want Charlotte to see me like this for it to be taken as an insult.' *I am mortified that anyone might think I had done this out of malice.*

Isabella had been equally moved by how her son's bride may look before the end of the year but that image had filled her heart with joy. 'You only wanted to show us how you attempted to disguise yourself while fleeing your abductor. Go to my son and let him see how you looked when he could only imagine it.' Isabella nodded to Rosemary to take Tony back to Caleb's bedroom as the rest of them headed downstairs.

Having announced her return before opening the door, Tony's worries about her step-mother vanished as Caleb turned his head towards them as she and Rosemary entered. His breath caught in a sharp gasp. Holding out his hand towards her, he blinked several times as he drank in deeply her attire. His hand caressed lovingly over Tony's baby bump as she stood in front of his arm chair.

'Oh yes my beautiful elfling, you'll be a very ugly mother!' Caleb drawled. Tony burst into a gurgle of laughter but Rosemary looked shocked.

'It's all right Rosemary,' Tony reassured as she bent over to press a kiss against Caleb's lips. 'When Caleb asked me how I looked when I was forced to try on my step-mother's dresses after the first abduction, I said I looked ugly. When he saw me in a dress for the first time Caleb teasingly said, "Yes very ugly." So he really isn't insulting me. Well I hope not!'

A note of doubt had entered her voice as she looked down into her fiancé's face. His dazzling smile reached his eyes as he drew Tony onto his lap.

'I don't know if I'd ever dare to do that elfling, I know you have a right hook that could break my nose.' Caleb laced his hand beneath her hair and drew her lips down to meet his. When it looked like the kiss was going to develop into something much more passionate, Rosemary cleared her throat.

'Before you get too carried away my Lady, you should change back into your normal dress so that I can unpack the baby bump. Your good dress may need to be washed and pressed to get the creases out of it.'

Reluctantly Caleb lifted Tony to her feet. 'Return my blushing bride to me as soon as you can Rosemary.' He captured Tony's hand before she moved too far away from him and seductively raised it to his lips. 'I like this look on you Tony, but there is one look that I'm aching to see again.'

It was her turn to drag in a sharp excited hiss of breath as her body flushed in desire. Rosemary looked puzzled from one to the other.

'But you haven't seen the wedding dress before my Lord.'

Releasing Tony's hand Caleb chuckled. 'What I had in mind involved a great deal less material!'

Before Rosemary could question him further, Tony dragged her out of the room as she whispered his desires into the Maid's ear. Gasping in surprise Rosemary was heard to say, 'Oh my Lord, you are very naughty.'

That caused Caleb to laugh and dwell pleasantly upon their past romantic dalliances until Tony was returned to him.

Mary's And William's Options

By early evening William and Mary were once more attending to their duties. When Tony finally managed to pin them both down to talk about the future, she found it hard to get their complete attention. It was not until Tony said firmly, 'This is important!' that the two servants stopped tidying up Caleb's room and sat down on the edge of Caleb's bed as instructed.

'Mary, when I'm married, I would love you to come with me to Delacourt Hall.' Tony caught the quick look between Mary and William but would not let them interrupt. 'Let me say my piece and then you may go and discuss all your options.' When the servants nodded, Tony continued, 'Caleb has a position available for William. His Butler is getting on in age and in a couple of years will retire. In the meantime he could do with some assistance and someone he can train to eventually replace the Butler. It won't be that much further to your families but if you prefer to stay here, Mary, you'll have to consider what position you could fill once I leave. You'd have to discuss your options with Mrs Preston.'

Caleb rose out of his chair and came over to stand behind Tony and wrapped his arms around her waist. 'There are another couple of options open to you. If you have any interest in living in London, at the moment my mother has the run of the town-house and is looking for good reliable staff. I expect we'll be going to London a little more regularly once we're finally married so it would be nice to know that we'd be leaving the London house in capable hands. If you're interested in getting married soon then either Stirling or I have tenant allotments if you want to settle down and start a family.'

Twisting sideways, Tony beamed up at Caleb. 'You've really put some thought into this since we talked about it!' She caressed her fingers down his still-bearded cheek before turning back to the shell-shocked couple sitting in front of them. 'You need time to think about what you want to do with your own lives. Also coming with me won't mean you and William can't be married. Go and discuss it together but Mrs Preston knows all about it and is more than willing to advise you.'

Jumping to her feet, Mary wrung her hands together in indecision. 'Oh my Lady, I can't leave you!'

Tony's eyebrows rose. 'Do you mean right now or ever? If you mean right now Caleb will feel slighted that you don't think he's capable of protecting Aidan and I. If you're worried about my reputation, please don't as I have nothing left regardless of how noble Caleb may have been!'

His arms tightened around Tony. Chuckling, he drawled, 'Thank you elfling! Between you and Doctor Masters I'm starting to doubt that I can be naughty.'

Turning in his embrace, Tony wrapped her arms around his neck. 'Oh, I know you can be very naughty! For now, though, let the world think you've been a saint.' She kissed him briefly as his lips quirked into a mischievous smile.

'A saint or a fool?' Caleb retorted, stealing another kiss.

She looked up at him a little sternly. 'If you were a fool then I wouldn't be prepared to marry you!'

Mary smiled. 'You asked for that my Lord. But before you become too engrossed in your battle of wits, I had meant I couldn't leave your service ever. That was my heart talking, you are correct, Will and I need to talk this through.' Holding her hand out to William, Mary excused them from the room.

The Earl's London Visit

Caleb only managed to secure one more kiss before they were interrupted again this time by the arrival of the Earl. The couple drew apart unhurriedly as Earl Stirling sank wearily into one of the arm chairs. Tony poured her father a glass of ginger ale, placing it into his hand before sinking onto the trundle bed beside Aidan as Caleb sat opposite the Earl in the other arm chair.

'We didn't expect you back tonight Papa,' Tony was a little concerned by the Earl's drawn features. He gulped down his cordial and shuddered at the memory of his very brief visit to London.

'Baby girl, it was impossible for me to remain in the metropolis a moment longer! I don't know where the information is coming from but London is a buzz with your story. Nigel was a handful all the way up to the city. The press already know that you're back and are camped outside our house in Mayfair.'

'I found no one of intelligence at the appropriate authorities and thought I must still be speaking another language. Until a senior officer rescued me from the dross and I managed to relay your story. Preston is seeing to it that he has something to eat before this man comes up to talk to you. Bell is his name.' The Earl paused for another drink. 'And then I had to inform Agnes about Claude's death.' Another shudder and Caleb was musing, hopefully *Agnes Henry has not also journeyed down to Stirling Manor with the Earl.*

Rising to collect the jug from the desk to refill her father's glass Tony said, 'Poor Papa! You didn't bring her back here did you?'

The Earl shuddered at the thought of being locked in a carriage with his mother-in-law for that length of time. 'No, thank God! I took Patrick and Officer Bell with me to tell Agnes. Just in case she inadvertently revealed she had known of Claude's actions or indeed planned it.' He paused for another sip.

'Did she betray any involvement?' Caleb asked He took Tony's hand as she sat down again.

'You suspected her?' The Earl was momentarily distracted from his tale.

'If it weren't for Nigel insisting that Aidan also be taken from the Manor. Neither of us thought Agnes could dare risk losing a Henry blood heir to Stirling. Claude revealed in Dieppe that his role was to secure Aidan's return and have the rest of us murdered.'

Sighing, Tony added, 'It was a huge risk to take as Nigel could've killed us all before Claude found us.'

Earl Stirling scrubbed his hand across his face as he placed his glass down on the table beside him. 'Well the news of her son's death didn't make her break her silence if she were involved.'

Tony shot a look of surprise at her father. 'She didn't react at all?'

The Earl shuddered again. 'Oh she reacted! Agnes screamed like a banshee, tried to scratch my eyes out and it took the combined effort of Bell and Patrick to drag her back and hold her in a chair while her Maid dosed her with some Brandy. It was several minutes before Agnes was calm enough for the men to release her and for me to explain what had happened in Dieppe.'

'Papa, would you like something stronger that cordial?' Tony offered as the Earl was obviously distressed by reliving his ordeal.

Laying his hand over hers, Earl Stirling managed a weak smile. 'Preston is organising a cup of tea for me.'

Right on cue there was knock on the door and Preston, himself, brought up a tea tray and laid it on the table beside the Earl. As the Butler bowed out of the room, Tony removed her hands from under Caleb's and her father's to pour the Earl a cup of strong tea. Respectfully the three young people in the room remained silent as Earl Stirling took several satisfying sips of his beverage. While on her feet, she poured out glasses of cordial for Aidan and Caleb before resuming her seat beside Aidan.

Sighing, the Earl finally lowered his cup to his lap before he continued, 'Agnes demanded to see Claude's body. Bell took her to the morgue but not before she threatened to destroy you for robbing her of her darling boy.' As he took another sip, he studied Caleb's face and wasn't really surprised that his future son-in-law was not in the least worried about Agnes' threat.

'Do you think she and Claude are behind the press knowing of our adventures? How much do the newspapers know? Did their information dry up with Claude's death?' Tony asked.

The Earl shook his head. 'They knew you were all back in England and that I was in London. Patrick was with me nearly the whole time so does that rule him out? I've left Patrick in London as he's going to discover what is being said by society and look into how the information is being leaked.' Neither Tony nor Caleb replied as they didn't have the Earl's faith that his nephew wasn't somehow involved. Their silence was more deafening than any words could have been. *I know that no speech of mine will convince them, we will just have to wait for Patrick to prove their doubts wrong.*

Interviewing The French Visitors

Officer Abraham Bell allowed them to eat their dinner in peace and surprised their French visitors by asking for their statements. They were gathered together in the morning room and Andre Guillaume voiced their confusion.

'We're more than willing to do anything to help but you'll be unable to prosecute Sutherland for anything that happened the moment they all set foot on French soil.'

'Firstly Mr Guillaume may I say how much I enjoy your stories. My two boys are now old enough to read your books.' Bell sat back comfortably in his chair with his note book open on his knee. 'By having the full story of what Lady Antonia and her entourage were forced to endure while in France will be a forceful argument for the prosecution to the instigators' intent to put them in extreme peril. The fact that Sutherland wasn't able to murder them does not diminish the danger that they were in.'

Rosemary had difficulty following Bell's broad accent and needed Louise to translate as Andre was acting as spokesman.

'Yes I see. Simply abducting them again was about humiliating them. Taking them and keeping them from leaving a hostile country is clearly intent to see them dead. Would you like us to write down our accounts so that you don't have to struggle taking notes?' asked Andre.

'Much appreciated Mr Guillaume, especially as the pretty little Miss is having trouble with my northern drawl.' Bell rose to his feet, prepared to give them some time to work without him breathing down their necks. *I'm not certain as to the others' ability to write in English and it will probably be necessary for Andre to write for all of them.* With that thought in mind, Bell paused as he opened the parlour door.

'Oh and Mr Guillaume, please remember that you're not writing a novel now, just the facts. Leave the descriptive prose for the book.'

Andre laughed and raised a hand in a fencing gesture to acknowledge a hit.

Officer Bell Meets The Masqueraders

When Bell was announced, as Charles, the Footman, opened the door of Caleb's room, the Bow Street Runner was a little amazed by the scene he encountered. Aidan was in his nightshirt already, with his fur rug being used as a cape as he bounced upon Caleb's bed. Tony stood in front of Caleb who was seated in an arm chair as she unwound his bandages to tend to his burns and bullet wound.

Tony paused and looked up as Bell entered the room but without turning around, she asked her brother to get off the bed or they might all end up sleeping on the floor. That caused Bell's eyebrows to rise in surprise but the officer was keeping his eyes on Caleb, whose hand covered his pistol. Not until Caleb had relaxed his stiff posture and removed his fingers from his weapon did Bell judge it safe to approach. Sighting a stranger, Aidan leapt off the bed and slipped around his sister's skirt, inserting himself comfortably onto Caleb's lap. Tony continued to remove Caleb's dressings.

'I hope you don't mind if I continue Mr Bell, but I'm trying to keep my brother to a strict routine.'

Bell bowed his head in acknowledgment. 'Please do go on, my Lady. Does Lord Delacourt object if I look at his wounds?' He moved closer now that Caleb had his hands full of a worried little boy rather than his weapons.

'Not at all. I suppose you've seen enough bullet wounds and burns in your line of work.' Caleb moved Aidan slightly so the boy sat more on his thigh than on his groin and wrapped him up in his rug.

'Aye that I have my Lord, but I'm betting it doesn't diminish the pain you're in.'

Cleaning, anointing and re-dressing Caleb's wounds Tony didn't object to Bell standing by her shoulder but thought his time might be better utilised elsewhere. 'I've written up our account to save you time, Mr Bell. I thought you could read through it and ask us any questions if we've forgotten anything.'

Moving towards the desk where several sheets of paper were covered with neat, elegant writing, Bell smiled, 'Do I make you nervous Lady Antonia?'

As she began to wind a bandage over the dressings that now covered Caleb's forehead, bullet graze and eyes once more, Tony didn't look up at the officer. 'No sir but as I said I like to keep my boys to a strict routine and it will very soon be time for my brother to have his medicine and go to bed. We arrived home very late last night or should I say very early this morning so the sooner Aidan is back to a regular bed time the quicker he'll recover fully.'

Picking up the pages, Bell paused as he considered her words. 'Oh aye, the Earl said something about Lord Aidan becoming ill so that you couldn't return home immediately. His Lordship didn't go into details but was it very serious?'

At that moment Tony cast a quick glance over her shoulder at him. 'Yes, it still is!' By the edge in her voice, Bell knew to not press that subject and sat down in the high backed chair beside the desk to read through Tony's notes.

Descending Back Into Darkness

Ignoring the Bow Street Runner for a moment, Tony knelt down in front of Caleb and taking his hands between hers, she waited for him to tell her what he needed as his return to darkness might be felt as a step backwards. Caleb's chest heaved as he dragged in a deep steadying breath to conquer his fear of the darkness. He removed his hands from Tony's and slid his around her waist, drawing her up onto the arm of his chair, clear of Aidan on the other side of his lap and laid his cheek against her breasts.

She tenderly wrapped her arms around his shoulders as he struggled to regain mastery over his demons. Placing a loving kiss on the top of his head, Tony caressed one hand lightly against Caleb's other cheek. Looking up from the notes, Bell was struck by how much strength each member of this tight unit gave to the others. *I'm not sure if that can be truly said about Lord Aidan.* Until the boy started to wriggle causing Lord Caleb to raise his head and take in a deep breath, finally regaining control over his weakness.

'Sorry Little Bear, are we crushing you?' Caleb reached out to run his hand over the boy to make sure that he hadn't sat Tony on top of him.

'No Papa... Caleb... I have to pee.' The tension left Caleb's body as his lips eased into a smile. Tony rose off his lap but Caleb refused to let her take Aidan from him.

'That's all right, the walk will do me good. You can keep Mr Bell entertained.' He rose, still holding Aidan in his arms. 'You'll have to guide me, Little Bear, so I don't walk into any doors.' They managed to reach the door without any major incident so long as Caleb stopped when told to and realised that "left one step" was more one of Aidan's steps than his own.

Too Clinical

Having watched their progress out the door, Bell looked back to find that Tony, now seated in Caleb's chair, was calmly watching him. Clearing his throat, he held up his handful of papers.

'You write a clear and concise account, my Lady.'

'But?' Tony gently prompted.

'It lacks what you were thinking and feeling. Don't get me wrong, you've explored the danger and the urgency but the personal anguish is missing. Don't you care that your reputation is almost completely destroyed? How did it make you feel that these people recklessly endangered your brother's health? Could have robbed your fiancé of his sight, of his life? Of yours?'

Slowly she nodded. 'I see, you want a victim's impact statement along with the clear cut facts of the events. I was trying to be rational and unemotional in my account and therefore unfortunately removed the soul within us all.'

Bell was glad to see that she was neither going to take offence nor render him uncomfortable by creating a scene. Reading some of his relief on his face, Tony smiled.

'Afraid I was going to start crying or screaming Mr Bell? What have you heard about me?'

Spreading his hands expressively he was not certain how to answer. 'Well I was a little surprised by your attire when I arrived this evening, my Lady. I had been told that you were usually seen in male clothing.'

'Yes what you see is my family's attempt to make me conform at last to society's expectations for someone of my breeding.' Tony drawled as she swept a hand elegantly down her gown covered body. 'For many, many years guilt has made me attempt to be the son and heir that my father needed. I dressed like a boy, acted like a boy and tried to think like a boy. I was naturally deluding myself but it also meant that I was not in the habit of crying, fainting, having the vapours or screaming like a banshee. That is why I took all female emotion out of the account. I feared it would cloud a straight forward narration.'

'I see,' Bell put the papers back down onto the table before continuing. 'How do you feel about the loss of your reputation?'

Tony took a deep breath and let it out slowly before she answered, 'For me, I don't care what people want to think or say about me. For my father and grandparents, I do care how it affects the family name and how it hurts them. I'm worried about how it will affect Caleb and his mother who have been dragged into this mess. I do wonder if this scandal will continue to haunt us and will have a negative effect upon our children and grandchildren if I'm blacklisted forever by all society.

Nodding, Bell was pleased. 'Put that emotion in your victim impact statement as you called it and we'll have the case sewn up tight.'

How Much Trouble Are We In?

Hearing Caleb and Aidan coming down the passageway, Tony quickly asked Bell, 'What trouble are we looking at over Claude's death?'

Bell's eyebrows rose. 'There'll be a coronial enquiry after the autopsy, but there's no doubt the Coroner will rule it as self-defence. Even if it wasn't, I don't see any jury in any country convicting a blind man who had just been shot by the deceased and was trying to protect his fiancée and her young brother.'

Tony sighed in relief. 'Good, the less we have to parade this scandal through the courts the better. I suppose you should also see Doctor Masters for a report of our injuries.'

'Yes my Lady, the Earl had a message sent to the Doctor on our arrival and…,' Bell drew out a pocket watch on a fob chain to check the time. 'I'm due to see him anytime now. So if you'll excuse me.' He opened the door to allow Caleb and Aidan to enter the room.

'Of course, thank you Mr Bell. I'll have the more emotional account written up for you before you leave in the morning.'

Bell bowed but paused in the doorway to watch Tony take Aidan from Caleb and settle him down in his bed in front of the fire. As she measured out a dose of medicine, Aidan became fretful until Caleb reached down and laid a gentle hand on the boy's shoulder. The medicine went down without further fuss and Aidan was rewarded with a piece of chocolate to take away the taste. Quietly closing the door behind him, Bell smiled. *They really are a beautiful family and I hope that all their troubles are finally behind them.*

Still On The Alert

The Bow Street Runner wasn't the only one with that dream for a peaceful future and Tony, for one, was not prepared to relax her guard just yet. She made certain that Caleb had access to his pistols at all times, that there was one placed under Mary's pillow and another under her own.

They spent the evening quietly and Tony was pleased when Mary returned and stated that she and William had made a decision. The courting servants had no desire to reside in London or take up farming but they would like to get married and take up the offered positions at Delacourt Hall. Although Tony was relieved by this choice she told them that any time they changed their minds the other options would still be available.

Caleb said there was no need for William to stay awake to watch over their door, but he did want Mary to sleep on the spare bed in the room. When Tony asked why, he just gave his mischievous smile and said that it would help him continue being a saint. Tony blushed but didn't deny that it was hard not to give into their desires. So Mary tucked them up in bed together before settling in her temporary bed.

Aidan knew that at any time he could join his sister but he chose his bed by the fire for now. William, although he thanked Caleb for his chance to seek his own bed, was following the Earl's orders and he set up his chair, shot-gun and a book to while away the hours until dawn.

Trouble Sleeping

They weren't the only ones to opt for an early night after such a disrupted early morning and soon the whole household was surrounded by darkness, except for the passageway that housed their bedrooms. A silence settled over the Manor like a peaceful blanket and yet even with Tony curled up in his arms, Caleb found it hard to sleep. *I realise it would be useless to toss and turn which would only disturb Tony's slumber.* In actual fact it was his absolute stillness that caused her to stir and raise herself onto one elbow.

'Caleb? What is it? Are you in pain?' Tony whispered, as she placed her hand lightly upon his chest where a bruise was forming over his heart.

'Not really, I can't explain why I can't sleep. It's just… a sense that something… just isn't right!'

Her sigh brushed softly against his cheek. 'I know, a sense of impending doom! Something wicked this way comes. Have we forgotten something? Underestimated someone? When… when we were alone in France I knew with clarity who I could trust, believe in, rely upon. You and Aidan. I hoped and prayed that there were one or two people in France who might help us but if we had to go it alone then so be it. Being isolated here in your room I still feel I can't be positive about whom I can trust beyond this room.'

Trailing his hand slowly down Tony's arm, Caleb did not immediately answer. 'Yes, that's how I've been feeling. Both of our cousins for example. It's hard to have such doubts about people we thought we knew so well. Thought we could trust with our lives. Are we ever going to manage to completely trust them again?'

Reaching up she caressed her hand against his bearded cheek. 'I don't honestly know! I was even wondering… if we need to consider possibilities outside the family for the instigator or the information leak.'

'Do you mean one of the servants or even someone in the village? Surely Preston would know if there was any disharmony amongst the servants. Is there anyone else in the village who was making a play for your hand? Have you snubbed any possible suitors lately?' Although it was a serious question Caleb tried to keep his tone light and jovial.

Her fingertips moved sensuously down the column of his throat and slowly over his chest. 'Apart from Andre, there is only Patrick and Duncan. The latter did say he had always known that the path his career will travel would not at all suit me. So I don't think he harbours any real resentment towards me. All the other young men in this district tend to look on me as a brother and if they had secret yearnings, not many of them could be considered by Papa to be eligible for an Earl's daughter.'

Her caresses moved lower down Caleb's body causing his insides to knot up as her hand trailed over his taut stomach. 'We did have trouble with a previous Footman who Preston caught pilfering in the wine cellar. He was let go but the last we heard he was doing quite well at a winery in France.'

Caleb's body stiffened in part due to Tony's exploring touch but more because of what she had said.

'What was his name?'

Her hand paused over his stomach as she considered the question. 'Adam… I don't remember his last name, he wasn't here that long. William may know if you want the answer right now otherwise Preston is sure to remember. Do you think that supposedly being in France makes Adam a suspect?' Tony's forefinger traced a light pattern across his belly button.

'If he happened to be related to Nigel Sutherland then we could have the link we've been missing.'

'Oh!' It was a sad, drawn out sound and Tony's hand stopped again. 'Then we may have to look at Noah, the Groom. I believe he is either Adam's friend or relative. The only problem with that theory is that both Noah and Adam know that I'm female but Nigel didn't know that. Surely they would have told him if involved with the first abduction?'

Caleb sighed and shrugged his shoulders. 'As Reverend Gray said to me, it had become a habit to speak of you as a boy. Neither of them may have thought it necessary as everyone in the village already knew.'

'Thereby assuming everyone in the country must know the truth?' Tony marvelled as she trailed a hand down his thigh.

Tired Of Being A Good Girl

A deep, slow sigh passed through Caleb's lips as he reached down to secure Tony's hand beneath his. 'Are you trying to distract me elfling?' He brought her hand back up to rest on his chest.

'I was hoping it would relax you a little so that you could sleep,' she admitted, not certain if he was angry with her.

'Actually it makes me think very, very naughty thoughts about the very adult things I'd like to be doing with you.' Caleb's voice dropped to a sultry tone as he raised her wrist to his lips. He could easily imagine the blush that swept over Tony as he heard her gasp of excitement.

'Well, to be completely honest with you, my Lord, I'm becoming tired of being a good girl. I want you to teach me how to be very, very bad.' Sitting up, she was pleased to hear the hiss of Caleb's sharp inhalation as her words swept him straight back to their erotic play in Paris. 'First I want to feel your naked, muscular and fabulous body pressed against mine,' she continued as she swiftly stripped out of her nightgown and under garments.

'And then?' asked Caleb, eagerly sitting up so that she could remove his nightwear.

'Then I want to feel your hands and lips all over my body before I then do the same to you.' Their garments fell noiselessly to the floor but he held himself in check and didn't reach out to draw Tony into his arms.

'And then? What if we can't stop elfling? Do you understand how much I want you?' Chuckling softly, she brushed her hand down his naked torso and wrapped her fingers around his growing erection, extracting a sigh from Caleb.

'Probably as much as I want you!' Tony tore a moan from his throat as she continued to slowly stroke his penis. 'I know you wanted to be able to see the first time we make love but if now is the right time then so be it, my love. Whether it is tonight or tomorrow after the official ceremony, it doesn't matter because you are already my soul mate!'

Releasing his penis, Tony gently pushed Caleb back into his back and leaning over him, laid claim to his mouth beneath her own.

'My love!' Her words brushed lightly across his lips.

'My life!' His whisper was a little hoarse in desire as she kissed him again. His hands found her arms and trailed up to cup Tony's face and they said together.

'My salvation!' Their kiss became more passionate, more of a silent duel but when Caleb, returning his hands to her shoulders, tried to ease Tony onto her back, she resisted. Reluctantly she released his mouth.

'No, please let me worship you first. Take the edge off your craving.'

A slow, sexy smile appeared on his face and although Tony couldn't see it properly, she heard it in his voice. 'My beautiful elfling, the final joining of our bodies does worry you doesn't it?' There was amusement but also understanding in his words and it only made her love him more.

'A little,' she admitted, 'but I do want to worship my own god-like husband.' She pressed a kiss against his jaw and then the side of his throat. 'To show you that I will always want to touch you and be touched by you.' Her next kiss was against the bruise over his heart before she began to trail her lips and caressing hands slowly down Caleb's responsive, aroused body.

They had no need for the bedding as their passion heated their skin and Tony gently eased the sheet back as she sensuously kissed down towards Caleb's taut stomach. *I'm not sure where I get the strength from to remain still as she slowly lavishes adoration upon my body.* Bunching the sheet beneath his hands, Caleb fought against the urge to overpower Tony, throw her onto her back and lay claim to all the glory that awaited them. *Would her instinct be to fight enough control to ensure that she is properly prepared for my first heart stopping thrust? Can I rock Tony's world without disturbing the slumber of the other people in the room?*

When Tony's soft, tender lips pressed against his penis, Caleb forgot how to think. As her hand slid between his legs to caress the hair over his thighs and her tongue trailed an erotic pattern over his erection, his lungs seized as he dragged several deep breaths in before he would pass out. When Tony's fingers played lightly with his balls and her warm, moist mouth descended to take his penis deep between her lips, Caleb fought to remain conscious.

Reaching out one, slightly unsteady hand, he located Tony's thigh as she lay in the opposite direction to him and slid his hand across her naked flesh until he cupped her backside. As Tony caressed her mouth along his hard, throbbing penis, Caleb eased his hand up over her hip and between her thighs. He was pleased with how damp she was already and that she willingly parted her thighs, moving the top one across his arm to allow him easier access to her hidden treasures.

When his thumb settled upon her clitoris and his first two fingers slid seductively lower into her vagina; Caleb experienced an absolute thrill rush through him as he felt Tony's sigh of pleasure reverberate against his genitals. Hazily, as he pumped his fingers into Tony in time with her sucking his cock, Caleb wondered, *is it possible for Tony to slide over my body so that I can use my mouth on her until she orgasms just as she is doing to me?*

As if Tony had heard his thoughts, she slowly removed her lips from around his swollen gland. 'Roll onto your side towards me. It's not the graze side of your head is it?'

Caleb dragged in a shuddering breath. *My God is she actually offering herself to me?* Swallowing hard, he removed his fingers from her vagina and as she moved back slightly, he rolled onto his side. His trembling hand eased her leg carefully over his shoulder and breathing in deeply of her arousal, Caleb lowered his head to take the delicate rose bud of her clitoris between his lips.

Extracting a whimper from Tony, he ran his hands along her heaving flank and moulded them around her breasts. Her body jerked as Caleb's tongue flicked sensuously against her moist passage and she lowered her mouth once more upon his penis to muffle her moan of desire. In the darkness, with soft sighs and low moans they pleasured each other. The scent of the other's arousal was as intoxicating as the caresses they received.

Sensing her own orgasm about to blossom, Tony had enough brain function to know that she didn't want to bite down on Caleb's penis as she came. So sliding him out of her mouth, she wrapped her hand around his throbbing erection and stroked Caleb to ejaculate, biting down on the bottom lip to contain her cry as his wicked tongue brought her also to climax.

Did I Cross A Line?

For a moment they lay there, breathing a little harder and savouring the pleasure that they had given and received. Placing a tender kiss against Caleb's thigh, Tony carefully eased her leg off his shoulder, making certain that she didn't accidently touch his burns or his bullet graze. Once they had disengaged, he rolled onto his back, dragging in a deep breath and held his arms open for Tony as she turned up the right way on the bed. She slid naturally into his embrace, briefly kissed his lips before taking in a deep breath and snuggled into his shoulder.

'That was all right wasn't it?' There was a note of doubt and worry in her voice as she teased her finger tips through the hair on Caleb's chest.

'More than all right my elfling.' There was no disguising the laughter in his voice.

'No I meant… I wasn't being too forward was I? It isn't the way things are done are they?'

He didn't need his eyes to know that she was blushing all over. 'My love, it was exactly what I'd been thinking about. I thought you must have read my mind.' He pressed a tender kiss against her forehead before lowering his lips to her cheek. 'Besides which,' he added, 'when have we ever done anything the way others expect it to be done? I thought you wanted me to teach you to become a very bad girl? Therefore there should be no restraints if you have the urge to try something new or different.'

Rolling Tony onto her back, Caleb went with her, careful not to crush her beneath him. Yet.

'Oh but you'll tell me if I cross the line won't you?' She was still filled with doubt about giving in to her desires. He pressed a kiss against her jaw and then her collarbone as his hands slid from her shoulders and cupped her breasts.

'Yes elfling. I thought that perhaps in this area I would be the master.' His kisses trailed down her chest towards her taut nipples and extracted an excited gasp form Tony as her body rose into his caress. 'But it would seem that we both have a lot to learn,' he added.

I Want More… I Want It All!

She threaded her fingers through his hair as hot, sensual kisses rained across her delicious breasts and his hand continued down to her waist. *The fire has barely died down within me and I'm astonished that I can yearn for it again so soon.* Releasing one hand from his hair, she slid her hand along Caleb's arm until she reached his hand poised over the apex of her thighs. *No I don't want it again… I want more!*

'Caleb…' Tony's chest heaved as she struggled to find enough breath to speak.

'Too soon?' He had misunderstood her reason for stopping the descent of his hand over her sensitised flesh. She swallowed hard as she struggled to get the words out.

'No, I want more… I want you… when you're capable to continue.' Her hand left his and slid between their bodies until she closed around his penis. It twitched in response to her touch and caused Caleb to drag in a sharp breath as he'd never had that quick a recovery rate as he seemed to have with Tony.

'Are you sure elfling? I'll understand if you want to wait until as you put it, "it is my ring you're wearing." I don't want you to ever regret anything we do together.' He felt a little disappointed as Tony removed her hand from around his penis to trail her fingers up his torso until she caressed his cheek.

'Am I likely to scream in pain?'

Caleb felt the doubt in her voice. 'I'm told it can be a sharp sudden pain but although you'll be a little sore for a day or two, it shouldn't be agony. Are you worried about making too much noise and waking Aidan and Mary? Because you will scream.'

Now confused, Tony shook her head. 'But you just said I won't scream in pain.'

Sliding his hand over hers, Caleb pressed her palm against his lips. 'I did but when you orgasm with me inside of you, it is highly probable that you will scream in pleasure.'

Her breath caught in a gasp. 'Oh! But I didn't scream just now.'

Caleb smiled. 'Yes but consider what we've done so far has only been the appetiser. When we get to the main course, the orgasm will be even more powerful!'

'Oh!' Just imagining that pleasure's magnitude caused Tony to lose her power of speech for a moment. 'Wow! We might even wake up the whole household in fright.' There was awe and yet also regret in her voice as her body had begun to melt against Caleb at the thought of an even more intense pleasure under his masterful Tutoring. Chuckling he bundled her back into his arms.

'Certainly Aidan wouldn't understand that I wasn't hurting you.' His calming reasoning brought a sigh to her lips.

'You'll find a solution after the ceremony won't you?'

He smiled as her attempt to sound nonchalant and hide her eagerness. 'Of course elfling!'

You're Bleeding Again

Brushing her fingers against his bearded cheek Tony drew her hand away in surprise. 'Are you crying? Your cheek is wet.'

Sighing, Caleb took her hand and licked it. 'No, that's blood,' he explained.

Tony immediately sat up. 'But I was so careful about touching your head!' She reached for the candle beside their bed and lit it as Caleb raised himself onto his elbow.

'Probably due to you raising my heart rate and pumping more blood around the old circulation rather than accidently touching the bullet wound.'

Tony slid off the bed and padded quietly across the room to where the medical bag sat on one of the arm chairs. She jumped startled and nearly dropped the bag when Mary spoke.

'What's wrong, my Lady? Are you needing my assistance?' There was a creaking as the Maid threw back her bedding and rose from her cot.

'Oh! How you scared me Mary! Sorry, did lighting the candle wake you?' Tony took the medical bag to the main bed and lit another candle beside Caleb so that she could clean up his injury. Instinctively, Caleb drew the sheet over the lower half of his body, forgetting that Mary had already seen both of them naked.

'No my Lady, I woke when you started talking.' Mary unwrapped his bandages as Tony removed the medical supplies she needed from the bag.

'**Started** talking?' Caleb laid emphasis upon the first word.

'Yes my Lord, when Lady Tony asked if you couldn't sleep due to pain.'

Tony felt a blush spread swiftly across her naked body but it was Caleb who spoke as Mary wiped away the blood oozing down his face.

'Then you heard everything? Oh no! Please tell me Aidan is still asleep!'

Tony glanced briefly over her shoulder to where the five year old lay snuggled under his fur rug. 'He seems to be asleep,' she reassured as she returned her attention to assist Mary re-dress his wounds.

'Yes my Lord, I heard everything. I would have put a stop to your love making if I thought it inappropriate but it wasn't.'

A sigh from Caleb suddenly made him seem so much older. 'Because we stopped from fully committing ourselves to the final consummation?'

Mary paused in the act of applying a fresh bandage and looked at him in surprise. 'No Lord Caleb. After your adventure in France it doesn't matter if you consummate your relationship now or after you sign a piece of paper; you're already bound together. I'm glad you did stop when you realised that it could affect Lord Aidan's fragile state of mind.'

A shade embarrassed that they had permitted their overwhelming desire for each other to override their care of

Aidan, both Caleb and Tony made no protest as Mary assisted them to re-dress in their nightwear before she tucked them back into bed.

'Are you angry with us Mary?' Tony asked as she took the Maid's hand.

'Of course not Lady Tony! I'm surprised at how long you've managed to resist the obvious passion that exists between you. I would've taken Father Jean Paul's offer to wed before the trek to Paris. I admit that staying in character and your brother's presence probably helped to keep you in check. I'm proud of you, all three of you and I'm so happy that you can finally be content with the gender God gave you.' Mary placed a tender kiss against Tony's forehead before she blew out the candle.

'Thank you Mary.' Tony curled up in Caleb's arms and suddenly felt very tired.

An Agonising Wait

Moving silently around the bed, Mary bent over to blow out the other candle but Caleb suddenly sat up, his hand latching onto the Maid's arm.

'Wait! There's something moving about outside,' he whispered.

'William would have called out if someone was in the corridor my Lord,' Mary tried to soothe as she eased his grip around her wrist.

'Not inside, Mary, outside of the house! They're going to try to get in through the window!' Caleb reached for his pistols as the two women listened hard for what he had heard. Mary gasped as they caught a faint thud as a ladder was leant against the wall.

'Do you want me to put out the candle?' Mary rushed back to her bed and drew out from under her pillow the pistol that they had placed there earlier.

'No, if either of you has a clear shot, take it,' ordered Caleb as Tony located her own pistol.

It was an agonising wait. With one trembling hand wrapped around her pistol, Mary's other hand was clenched so tightly into a fist that her fingernails dug painfully into the palm of her hand. Glancing across at the two very still figures on the bed Mary noted that Tony had relit the candle beside her.

Their calmness at yet another attack upon them I find un-nerving. There is no panic, no need for hurried instructions, no attempt to hurry Lady Tony or Lord Aidan to safety and no desperate tearing away of his bandages so that Lord Caleb can see. More than once he has defended his family while blind so he is not disturbed by his lack of sight now. For the first time I am experiencing the tension and fear they not only endured for five days in France but since they first encountered Nigel Sutherland.

Briefly, very briefly Mary noticed Tony glance away from the window to the cot by the fireplace where her brother lay. *Almost I can see what my mistress is thinking. If any of them shoot the intruder through the closed window that window would in all likelihood shatter and cold air would rush into the room. That could further endanger the young Lord's fragile health.*

Without really being aware of her actions Mary flung her pistol onto the bed beside Tony, drew Juliette Martin's fur coat off the back of an arm chair and threw it over the top of the sleeping boy before picking up the long handled bed warmer which sat beside the fire place. As a head and a hand carrying a pistol appeared at the top of the ladder, Mary flung open the window.

'No! You'll not harm my children!' Mary snarled as she swung the bed warmer up over her head and brought it down with all her might upon the intruder's head. There was a clang as the bed warmer made contact, a colourful oath in pain, a scream as the intruder lost his grip on the ladder and fell backwards, then finally a thud as he hit the ground hard. Her breast heaving

in extreme emotion, Mary shut the window as William, startled
by Mary's war cry, burst into the room.

As Caleb's pistols turned towards him, William stuttered,
'It's William, my Lord!' When the weapons were lowered, the
Footman took another step into the room. 'What's happened?'
William was surprised to see that Mary was shaking.

'Mary knocked out someone trying to get in via the
window,' Tony explained, laying her pistols down as she rose
from the bed to wrap a shawl around the Maid's shoulders.

'Shall I go and have a look outside, Lady Tony?' William
lowered his shot gun with the immediate threat neutralised.

'No, there could be a second attempt from within the house
if you leave.' Tony shook her head as she eased Mary into one of
the arm chairs. Casting a quick glance out the door, William said,
'Two people are approaching, Monsieur Guillaume and Mr Bell.'

Some of the tension left Caleb's body. 'Take Andre
downstairs and check on the intruder, let us know if you
recognise him. Officer Bell can take your place here.'

'Of course my Lord.' Handing his gun to the Bow Street
Runner, William collared Andre and they headed out to see if the
intruder were alive or dead.

The Household Is Roused

Abraham Bell quietly closed the door, leaving Tony to
comfort an upset Mary, a gentle woman who had never done
anything so violent in her whole life. Just then he saw the Earl
hurrying down the corridor towards them.

'Your father is coming, Lady Antonia,' Bell stuck his head
back into the room.

'Thank you Mr Bell, let him in. Oh, I should have told
William to send someone for Doctor Masters in case the
intruder is still alive.' Tony looked up at Bell, clearly distressed
she hadn't thought of the man's welfare.

'We can see to that when we know you're safe, my Lady.' Bell bowed and stood aside as Earl Stirling breezed past him in a very ornate brocade dressing gown.

'I thought it was all over, baby girl. Don't tell me Nigel Sutherland managed to escape again!'

'It's a long story, my Lord,' Caleb cocked his head slightly to one side. 'But I think we may be about to get some answers.' Sliding his hand across the bed, Caleb located Mary's and Tony's pistols and tossed one towards the Earl and the other towards Tony as she rose to her feet. The Earl took up a position in front of his son's bed as hurried footsteps approached down the passageway.

'Identify yourself young man,' Bell ordered, holding up his hand to halt the approach of a fully dressed servant. He was forced to catch his breath before he could speak.

'I'm Noah, one of the Grooms at the Manor. Is Lady Tony all right? I heard a scream.'

Bell cast a shrewd glance over the Groom's attire and deduced that he had not dressed in haste. 'Perhaps you'd better see for yourself.' The Bow Street Runner opened the door and gestured with his head for Noah to enter the bedroom. Noah had barely stepped inside when he felt the muzzle of Tony's pistol press against the side of his head.

'Make any move towards a weapon, Noah, and I will blow your head off!' Tony stated calmly. 'Mr Bell please come in and search him for any weapons.'

'I don't understand, my Lady, why would I be armed? I'm here to see if you're unharmed?' Slowly raising his hands, Noah turned to face Tony as Officer Bell slipped into the room beside them. The Groom looked like butter wouldn't melt in his mouth and Tony hadn't actually seen the features of the intruder before Mary had hit him.

Bell had seen his fair share of credible criminals and snorted in derision. 'You just happened to be fully dressed at this hour of night!' The officer quickly located a knife, a pistol and a cosh hidden on the Groom and threw them onto the bed out of Noah's reach.

'Well you are!' Noah retorted but Bell only chuckled.

'I've been expecting further trouble. Besides which you can't have got up here so quickly after your accomplice fell off his ladder. So what's your beef son? Are you and your mate just opportunists or are you involved with the previous attacks upon Lady Stirling and Lord Delacourt?'

A Family's Revenge

A sneer descended upon Noah's face as he pointed an accusing finger at the Earl. 'Ask his Lordship about what he made Adam do and then hung him out to dry?'

Earl Stirling looked startled. 'I have no idea what you're talking about! Adam who?' He had lowered his weapon as he stared at the Groom in surprise.

'Adam, the Footman dismissed for stealing alcohol from the wine cellar,' Tony received a snarl from Noah.

'You don't even know his last name! Just another lowly servant to take the blame for an aristocrat's sins! You forced Adam to supply you with alcohol on the sly and when Mr Preston found out about it you denied any involvement! Do you know how hard it has been for Adam to get a decent position after his dismissal?'

Caleb's eyebrows rose under his bandages. 'I thought you said he had found work in a winery in France, Tony?'

She wasn't listening as she stared tearfully at her father. It was Mary who explained.

'That is correct Lord Caleb. Adam had written to Polly, the Maid at the Rectory, that he'd found work more congenial to his tastes and once he was settled he was going to send for her.'

'Papa? Please tell me the truth? Have you been secretly drinking? Did you force Adam to procure alcohol for you and then let him be dismissed when he was found out?' Tony's voice was soft and filled with hurt. She thought she knew this man who now stood before her and she was valiantly trying to hold back the tears that threatened to fall at any moment. Caleb thought, *It would take a braver man than me to withstand a child whose faith had been completely shattered.*

'Yes and no, baby girl. I swear to you that I've had no one but Preston supply with me with an occasional stress release. Usually once a month when Charlotte becomes most psychotic during her monthly cycle. During the last three months, the first mouthful of wine I've had was the champagne at your engagement.'

A polite clearing of the throat announced the arrival of Preston, the Butler. 'Lord Stirling speaks the truth, Lady Tony. Also what I had been supplying his Lordship had been wine and not spirits which is what had been going missing when I caught Adam stealing. At first Mrs Hill had noticed that the kitchen supply of cooking sherry and brandy had been mysteriously disappearing. Once these were placed under lock and key, Adam had been caught breaking into the wine cellar of which I alone had the key.'

'How much has Papa been consuming at a time?' The tears were still close to the surface as Tony demanded in a faint voice to know the extent of her father's illness. Spying Adam's medicine and measuring cup, Preston strode across the room to hold up the small measuring cup to Tony.

'That much once a month if Lady Charlotte was being a little… irrational. After you were abducted a second time, a dose every day until your letter arrived from Paris stating you were all safe. I can't say with confidence whether the Earl needed a little something to cross the channel. I know that he and Lord Aidan don't travel well over open water.'

The Earl shook his head. 'Doctor Stevenson gave me some sort of tonic to prevent being sea sick. All natural herbs he promised. Tony, if that young man had been stealing for me, I would've owned up and ensured that he had a good position to go to but I've not touched spirits in over ten years. When I learnt that your grandfather had been drunk when he accidently drove his curricle off a cliff, I swore I'd never let alcohol rule my life as well.'

Burying his head in his hands the Earl sank into the arm chair opposite Mary. As her tears finally fell, Tony knelt down to wrap her arms around her father.

'Oh Papa, I'm sorry, I didn't know that you still struggled against your addiction.'

Leaving father and daughter to re-connect, Bell prodded Noah. 'Perhaps you'll answer my earlier question now, young man. Are you opportunists or part of the original abduction scheme? Are you involved with Nigel Sutherland?'

Noah sighed. 'Adam and I are brothers. Nigel is our step-brother. When Adam told us about the Earl's betrayal, Nigel came up with the abduction plan to humiliate the Stirling family. After Nigel was captured we received a letter telling us how to rescue Nigel and get him into the house for the second abduction.'

Looking up suddenly, Tony asked, 'Who sent you that letter? Who are you working for?'

Noah shook his head. 'I don't know, Adam never told me and he said he had been instructed to destroy the letter. Have you killed Adam?'

Tilting his head slightly to one side, Caleb heard footsteps coming down the passageway. 'We're about to find out now. I hear only one set of footsteps, is that Andre or William?'

Bell motioned Noah away from the door so that he could open it and stick his head out. 'It's Monsieur Guillaume.' He stepped back to allow Andre to enter.

Noah's Confusion

Glancing around the room, Andre was a little startled by the increase in the number of people in the room since he and William had gone outside.

'Your intruder is alive but his injuries look serious. William has arranged for one of the Grooms to ride into the village for your Doctor. We put the intruder into the morning parlour. I didn't think he'd survive being carried any further and especially not upstairs. William identified the intruder as an ex-Footman, Adam, who is asking for someone called Noah. Have I missed anything interesting? Are these two young men also competing for the hand of the lovely Lady Tony?'

Caleb sighed as Andre threw himself onto the bed beside him. 'Do you deliberately try to provoke me, Andre, when you know I'm armed and dangerous?'

The Author chuckled as he ran his hand along Caleb's arm. 'I only do it as I know I'll always get a rise out if you! So what's the plot? A new scenario or a continuation of the same story?'

Staring at Andre in equal measure of awe and puzzlement, Noah said, 'Continue,' before transferring his attention to Bell. 'May I go down to my brother? I need… if Lord Stirling is telling the truth… why would Adam lie to me if he really was guilty?'

Sympathetically Bell patted Noah's shoulder. 'In my line of work son, I see a lot of alcohol induced violence and criminal behaviour. Alcohol can be a nasty, demanding master once it takes hold of you. At first you might need it to take the edge off a bad day. Soon you need to increase the frequency and amount to alleviate the growing emptiness inside of you. Then it is all you can think about, you'll do anything, say anything to satisfy this addiction. It doesn't help that the Georgian era we live in, with its hard drinking and deep play, defines what it means to be a real man. Don't be too judgemental upon your brother, son, you may find that he's been lying to himself about his drinking as much as he has been lying to you.' Opening the door, Officer Bell gestured for Noah to leave the room but the Groom paused to look back at the Earl.

'I'm sorry, my Lord. I never dreamed that Adam would let this scheme for revenge go ahead if it were not true.'

Raising his head, Earl Stirling saw the regret in the Groom's eyes and nodded solemnly. 'I'll do what I can for you, Noah, but what you've done to my children, to my family is a serious business. It was only through their own ingenuity and some really good friends that my daughter wasn't raped and all three of them murdered.'

Noah's shoulders sagged. 'I didn't know that Nigel would become so angry he'd lose sight of the reason we were doing this. It should've been about the money needed for Adam to get back on his feet again. I didn't find out about the order to kill them all until after they had escaped from Nigel on the ship and he was already chasing them all over France.' Feeling Bell's hand gently at his elbow, Noah bowed and allowed the officer to lead him downstairs. Preston followed them to the door.

'If you don't need me, my Lord, I'll make certain that everything is ready for Doctor Masters when he arrives.' The Butler bowed and when Earl Stirling nodded Preston quietly closed the door.

No More Adventures?

For a moment there was only silence and then collectively, those present sighed in relief. A small voice came from beneath the fur coat.

'Caleb?'

'Yes Little Bear?' Caleb placed one of the pistols back under his pillow and the other on the bedside table.

'Can we go back to sleep now?'

Rising to her feet, Tony chuckled. 'As soon as we've sent Papa and Andre back to their own beds.' She placed the pistol still in her hand beneath Mary's pillow before hauling on Andre's arm to remove him from the main bed.

'How long have you been awake Little Bear?' Caleb felt Tony slip into bed beside him.

'When Tony asked you if you were still awake due to pain.' Aidan's head popped out of the fur as he pushed the coat away from his face.

'What!' Caleb nearly jumped out of his skin in horror that Aidan may have heard them making love. That was until he heard the boy giggle.

'I heard Mary say that and knew that it would be funny if I said it too.'

Groaning in disbelief but also in relief, Caleb buried his cheek against Tony's shoulder. Assisting the Earl to his feet, Andre glanced across at the engaged couple in interest.

'Have you two children been naughty again? Thank goodness you'll be married tomorrow before your passion causes you to burst into flames.'

With a sigh, the Earl linked his arm through the Author's. 'Please Andre that is my daughter you're talking about.'

Andre patted his hand sympathetically. 'I know Lord Stirling but I'm not the man who can't keep his hands off her!' He led the Earl towards the door.

'Good night gentlemen!' Tony said a little sternly. 'Aidan doesn't need anything else to give him nightmares!' *He certainly did not need to know about my sex life!*

'Can I…can I join you and Caleb now? Or are you going to be naughty again?' Aidan sat up and clutched his fur rug around him, Andre uttered a wicked laugh which earned him a censorious look from the Earl.

'Come on Little Bear.' Caleb patted the bed, 'We're all going to sleep now.'

Throwing off the fur coat, Aidan dragged his fur rug along with him as he jumped up into the main bed between Tony and Caleb. Having recovered from the shock at having perhaps killed someone, Mary rose to her feet and as Andre closed the door upon his and his host's departure, Mary finished tucking the trio up in bed together.

'Once you're married, Lady Tony, this isn't going to become the normal lifestyle is it?'

Caleb reached for Mary's hand as she blew out the candle beside him. 'Except for it being legal for my bride and I to be as naughty as we like, no I certainly hope that this will not become a way of life for any of us.'

Snuggling into the two people who meant the world to him, Aidan yawned. 'Couldn't we become pirates?'

Mary snuffed out the other candle as Caleb immediately answered and released the Maid's hand.

'Certainly not!'

'Why?' The small boy yawned again.

'Firstly we'd be in competition with Captain Sheppard and he wouldn't like that.' Caleb ran his hand over the top of the blanket until he located Aidan's head. 'Secondly you suffer from sea sickness and thirdly I need to look after my estate and you need to attend to your school work.' He smoothed a wayward curl out of Aidan's eyes.

'So no more adventures?'

Caleb could not help but smile at the thought that being married to Tony would be boring or uneventful. 'Just a different kind of adventure Little Bear. You'll probably have your new Tutor on the run just to keep up with you. If you think Tony and I are becoming boring and staid then we can arrange another adventure, perhaps though, a little less lethal than this one.'

Yawning and unconsciously bunching a handful of Caleb's nightshirt in his small fist, Aidan giggled. 'When you're not being naughty in every room in the house.'

An embarrassed gasp escaped from Tony. 'Oh no! You must have overheard me say that to Caleb on the yacht! Sorry Little Bear, that wasn't meant for your ears.'

The small lad only giggled again. 'It just means that we'll have to learn to knock on closed doors. Oh! When I'm told I've been naughty, it's because I've done something wrong or sinful. Is it the same when Andre says you've been naughty?'

Raising his hand to brush tenderly against Tony's cheek, Caleb could easily imagine her blush.

'Not quite,' he admitted, 'technically society dictates that what your sister and I have been doing should strictly be kept until after we are officially wed.'

Sighing, Aidan's hand tightened further upon Caleb's nightshirt. 'If you weren't going to marry Tony then it would be wrong?'

'Very ungentlemanly behaviour!' admitted Caleb as he leant forward to claim a brief kiss from Tony.

'That's all right then.' Aidan yawned and Tony rearranged his fur rug so that it covered her brother's head.

A delighted chuckle came from Mary as she lay back down on her own cot. 'Does he really understand what you two have been up to?'

Sighing Caleb located Tony's hand and entwined their finger. 'I hope not! At least not until he's older,' he admitted. 'Maybe in fifteen or twenty years' time when he falls passionately in love.' There was so much obvious doubt in his voice that Aidan might think any less of his new brother that Tony refrained from laughing.

'All that Aidan needs to understand is that here with us, he is perfectly safe.' Tony caressed her lips gently against Caleb's.

'Safe,' sighed Aidan, already half asleep, 'and sleepy.' Taking the hint that had been dropped with the subtlety of a boulder, silence descended over the room at last.

WEDNESDAY
I Might Keep The Beard

It is nice to wake up to normal. Well, as normal as we can achieve at this present time. Aidan is chafing at the bit at his continued confinement but I solemnly promised him that he can come to the wedding at the church if he stops jumping up and down on Caleb's bed. Especially as I'm trying to remove Caleb's bandages and attend to his burns. Accepting the terms of her deal, Aidan jumped off the bed and allowed Mary to dress him anyway she liked.

He was certainly more warmly attired than it was necessary for a usual Summer's day but Mary knew it was quite cool inside their little church. Tony closed the curtains and placed onto Caleb's face the dark but still see-through glasses that Doctor Masters had delivered before she allowed Caleb to finally open his eyes. Casting a supercilious glance at Tony over the top of his dark glasses, Caleb managed to control a smirk as one of his eyebrows rose.

'I don't wish to rain on your fashion sense, my elfling, but I hope that's not what you're planning to wear in church.' One hand reached out to tug on the long sleeve of Tony's nightgown as she completed securing a gauze pad over Caleb's bullet graze. 'I'm not complaining mind you, I mean I'd rather tear that gown off your body than the very expensive dress Andre told me you bought in Paris.'

Mary shot Caleb a warning glance but it was too late as Aidan had not been lost in his own dream world but paying close attention to his future brother.

'Why would you want to tear any clothing off Tony at all?'

59

Not even attempting to hide her smirk, Tony's gaze met Caleb's before he lowered his eyes to Aidan's.

'I'll leave you to explain that one, my Lord!' Tony sank into an elegant curtsy and would have moved away from the bed to pack up the medical bag but Caleb reached out to firmly grasp her hand and kept Tony by his side. Looking down into the boy's puzzled face, Caleb took a deep breath and decided that he was never going to lie to his little brother.

'The truth is Aidan…' manfully Caleb got that far when glancing up at the embarrassed face of Mary, Aidan realised the truth for himself.

'Oh, it isn't some sort of punishment but about being naughty.'

Caleb exhaled slowly, in relief mostly. 'Exactly Little Bear.'

The boy's brow puckered once again. 'But if you're married, why would it still be naughty?'

Unable to help it, Mary burst out laughing. Although she smiled, Tony was more serious as she answered, 'Well technically it won't be naughty.'

'Unless we get caught!' Caleb wrapped his hands around Tony's waist and drew her down onto his lap.

'Caleb, one more word from you and I'll let Mary shave you!' Tony warned as she patted her hand against his bearded cheek.

'Oh no my Lady!' protested Mary in horror. 'You know I don't have a steady enough hand with a razor.'

Caleb chuckled as he ran his fingers over his beard. 'Tony is well aware of that fact and it is why she suggested it. Do you know elfling, I think I might just keep the beard.'

Surprising Caleb by not reacting immediately to his provocation, Tony ran her fingers across his beard before finally leaning forward to press her lips against his ear.

'Not unless you want to contemplate a sexless marriage,' she whispered and felt his body stiffen immediately beneath her.

'Quickly Mary, my shaving gear!'

Satisfied she had made her point, Tony slid off his lap. 'William will help you shave and dress. Mary and I will be in my room next door.' Tony glanced across at Aidan. 'Do you want to stay and help Caleb or come with me?'

Slipping his hand under his pillow for a pistol, Caleb glanced across at the fire place where a fire had continued to burn all night.

'Your room probably won't be warm.' Caleb pressed the weapon into Tony's hand. 'Take this, just in case.' He kept his tone light as he thought, *being this close to everything I had ever dreamed becoming a reality, I am not prepared to take any foolish chances.* Nodding, she accepted the pistol and as William entered with hot water for Caleb's shave, Tony and Mary headed next door to the fantasy gown that awaited.

A Bastion Of Female Solidarity

It was on the recommendation of Doctor Masters that Earl Stirling did not tell Tony and Mary that Adam had died in the early hours of the morning. The Doctor felt this day should be one of celebration and not mourning. Announcing his presence, he entered to see Mary pause as her hand lowered to the pistol on the dressing table beside her. Dropping a brief curtsy the Maid returned to applying a hint of colour to Tony's lips.

Rosemary had been sitting on Tony's bed, surrounded by red roses as she entwined them into a wreath to sit upon Tony's long flowing hair. She managed to get to her feet to also curtsy without dropping her almost completed circle of roses. A bouquet of blood red roses intertwined with white rose buds lay already on the dressing table.

Only mildly surprised the Earl found his daughter's room a little more crowded than he had expected. Sitting in the arm chairs were his mother, Lady Margarette, and his mother in law,

Patience Sinclair. Tony's future mother in law, Isabella, sat on Tony's bed making up corsages to pin to the ladies' dresses and place in the men's lapels.

What does surprise me, mused the Earl, *is not only the fact that Aidan has stayed with Caleb but also that Charlotte and Lizzy are not also present at this bastion of female solidarity.* Quietly into the Dowager Countess' ears, the Earl asked if his wife and her sister had been asked to join the other ladies in Tony's preparations. Lady Margarette shot her son such a speaking look that he immediately wished he hadn't mentioned it.

'I'm afraid Charlotte ran out of here in tears as both Grandmama Sinclair and Lady Isabella said how much I reminded them of Mama.' Tony explained, trying to take the scornful sneer out of Lady Margarette's disapproving look.

'Oh well naturally they'd see it; one being Grace's mother and the other her best friend.' The Earl sighed and wondered, *Am I in for an overly emotional six months with Charlotte's fluctuating hormones? Especially now that Tony will be leaving the house.*

Completely her wreath of red roses, Rosemary handed it to Mary to carefully place it upon Tony's head before she was finally allowed to rise from her chair and turn to face her father. His Lordship's breath caught in his throat as his lungs tightened remorselessly around his heart.

The bright red of the roses are matched by not only Tony's lips but also the spectacular diamonds and rubies necklace and earrings on loan from my mother. The fairy tale dress in ivory reminds me of the numerous times that Tony and Grace played dress up together. As tears welled up in his eyes, the Earl could easily understand how Isabella and Patience had seen the mother in the daughter now standing looking worriedly at him.

'Papa? What is it? Are you ill?' Tony reached out for one of his hands as Isabella attached a rose to his lapel.

'I'm all right but I think we may have been too hasty in accepting that Caleb was the right man for you.'

Looking up from attaching a corsage to the Dowager Countess, Isabella said, 'Why is that Julius?'

The Earl managed to drag in a deep breath, 'Tony was obviously meant to be a princess!'

Shaking her head as she chuckled, Tony released her father's hand. 'But would I love anyone else the way I love Caleb? Just for today, perhaps, we should temporarily dub Caleb a Crown Prince?'

Isabella laughed. 'Well apparently in Paris Andre went looking for a costume to match Tony's dress and is trying to convince Caleb that he should wear it.'

The Earl's eyebrows rose. 'I'm surprised you're here Isabella and not with your son.'

'I was,' Isabella bent down to pin a corsage onto Patience's dress, 'but he said I was making him nervous.'

'Why?' Tony was suddenly worried for her beloved and was regretting having left his side for even a brief time. 'What happened?'

Looking up from attaching her own corsage, Isabella smiled. 'I'm not really sure. While Caleb was lathering up his face before shaving, I had been sitting in one of the arm chairs with Aidan upon my lap. I was telling Aidan about Delacourt Hall and some of the activities he might be interested in when you take him there for a visit. I didn't think we were talking too loudly or were a distraction but when Caleb glanced across at us as he raised a razor to his face, a strange expression crossed his features.'

'His hand shook so much that Caleb dropped the razor. He said the image of me playing with my grandson was a little too distracting so I offered to leave but I don't really understand it at all. Caleb was never so affected seeing me with his nephew and niece, Paul and Emily.'

The tension left Tony's body as she sighed in relief. 'Caleb was equally affected when I was cradling Aidan after we'd escaped from Nigel after the first abduction. We were in the stable on the Patterson's farm. He saw in the image me holding our own son one day like that.'

'Oh I see.' Isabella was visibly relieved as she attached flowers to Rosemary's and Mary's dresses. 'I was worried that Caleb hadn't quite recovered from your French adventure and still thought of Aidan as his actual son.'

Although the Earl looked shocked, Tony's face relaxed into a smile. 'The blurring of the lines between reality and the masquerade is probably what shook up Caleb.' Accepting, with thanks, from Mary her bouquet of red and white roses, Tony returned her eyes to her father's face. 'Do you want to see if Charlotte is able to come to the church with us?'

The Earl had extended his hand out to assist his mother out of her chair but now hesitated. 'My duty is to ensure that you safely reach the church baby girl.'

Tony's eyes twinkled as she glanced around at the other women in the room. 'A man would have to be very stupid to attempt anything when I'm surrounded by all my family.'

Lady Margarette's lips thinned as she fought to keep an acid retort about her daughter in law under her tongue. 'Go to your wife, Julius, if anyone else was to go it could be taken as a slight to her position. We have enough drama going on that we do not need to un-necessarily add to it!'

Crown Prince Material

With a resigned sigh, the Earl left his female relatives to escort Tony down to the entrance hall where Caleb stood, holding Aidan's hand. With them were Andre, Geoff, William and to Tony's surprise, Doctor Masters. When the men turned as the ladies approached, Tony noticed that Caleb's eyes had been bandaged once again and with a cry of anguish she slipped her hand out of the arm she had entwined with the Dowager Countess and rushed to Caleb's side.

'What has happened? Has your eyesight worsened?' Tony raised trembling fingers to caress against Caleb's freshly shaved cheek. Rosemary and Mary assisted Isabella to place a red rose onto the lapel of each of the gentlemen gathered.

'Don't panic elfling,' Caleb's calm tone soothed some of Tony's fears. 'Doctor Masters thought it prudent to cover up the burns when I'm outside.' Caleb took her hand and pressed her palm against his lips. Tony threw a quick questioning look across at the Doctor but he only smiled at her worried expression.

'The bandages will come off once you get into the church. Although a hat may have been enough to shade his Lordship's burns I was worried it would put unnecessary pressure against the bullet wound.'

Relieved by the Doctor's no nonsense tone, Tony sighed and took a step back to finally take in Caleb's costume. He wore an ivory shirt, over which was a blood red knee length tunic with a wide belt. Attached to the belt was a sword. Not the rapier sword Tony had been in the habit of wearing but a broad sword. Caleb had on under the tunic, skin tight buff breeches and shoes instead of his usual boots.

He looked absolutely delicious and as Andre scooped Aidan up into his arms and Tony slipped her hand into the crook of Caleb's arm to lead him out to the waiting carriages, she whispered into his ear just how delectable he looked. Laughing he laid his other hand over the top of hers.

'I was worried that I looked like a court jester,' he admitted, as he took his place in the carriage beside her and accepted Aidan from Andre.

Tony smiled. 'Definitely Crown Prince material.' As Isabella and Andre entered the carriage Tony kissed her soon-to-be husband.

'Mama, have I come into an inheritance that I don't know about? Or has the kiss of the beautiful princess turned this ugly frog into a prince?' Caleb's words caused Andre to laugh but Isabella looked a little surprised.

'Julius said that perhaps he should have sought out a prince for Tony as she looks like a princess in her wedding dress.' His mother explained before asking, 'How did you know I was in the carriage?'

Caleb smiled, 'Your unique perfume Mama, just as I know that Andre alighted with you because…' He wasn't permitted to finish as Andre warningly tapped his knee.

'Careful son, if you say because of my perfume, I'm going to punch you - bride groom or not!'

Shaking his head, Caleb's hand dropped to the broad sword at his side. 'Before you rudely interrupted I was about to say because of your wicked little laugh. Now what have I told you about provoking me when I'm armed?'

'One of these days son, we'll have the gloves off and we'll settle this once and for all!'

Laying her hand over Caleb's on the hilt of his sword, Tony sighed. 'Boys behave or I'll be the one dishing out the punishment.'

As the carriage door was closed she added, 'Where's Rosemary and Mary? I meant to ask Papa if the servants were allowed to attend the wedding.'

Isabella reached forward to take her free hand. 'Preston and a couple of armed volunteers are staying at the Manor so that there will be no nasty surprises when we return from the church. Otherwise all of the servants and villagers are permitted to attend the ceremony. Rosemary is helping the Dowager Countess into the Sinclair carriage and Mary is on the box beside our driver. Try to relax, everything has been taken care of.'

Returning the pressure of Isabella's fingers, Tony tried to smile. 'I just don't want anyone to feel left out. Oh, I haven't seen François and Louise this morning.'

Unable to help himself, Andre chuckled, 'They are already at the church, decorating the ends of the pews with flowers and arranging vases of red and white roses. You really are a micro-manager aren't you? Are you this controlling in bed?'

A gasp of surprise came not from Tony but Isabella. 'Monsieur Guillaume! That is a highly inappropriate question to ask, especially in front of Tony's brother!'

As the line of carriages and other vehicles had trundled down to the village, Aidan hadn't been paying any attention to what the adults had been saying. He had been absorbed in playing with the shiny buttons on his own jacket. Looking up now, Aidan glanced from Tony to Isabella.

'Doctor Masters said that if they had been a little naughty, they hadn't been very, very naughty.' Glancing up at Caleb, Aidan added, 'Caleb said it would've been wrong if he didn't intend to marry Tony so that means that he's a gentleman after all.'

Blushing, Caleb caressed his hand against the boy's hair. 'Thank you Little Bear.'

'Out of the mouths of babes!' laughed Andre but Isabella was still startled.

'Were you actually naughty in front of Aidan?'

The little boy sighed, bored now by the direction of the conversation. 'I never saw them do more than kiss. They were both clothed whenever I crawled into bed with them.'

Glancing across at Tony, Aidan asked, 'Mary said that Squire Perkin's Connie has had her puppies. So can I see them?'

'Tomorrow or the next day depending on when Doctor Masters says you're well enough.' Tony paused briefly before adding, 'Connie is a Jack Russell, Aidan, and I thought you wanted a puppy that could grow up to protect you?'

Solemnly Aidan nodded but suddenly his cheeky dimples appeared. 'I still want that but I just like to play with puppies; any kind of puppies.' Chewing thoughtfully on his inner cheek,

Aidan added, 'And kittens. I like kittens too but their claws are a little sharp. I would like to have a tiger but I'd be worried that he'd want to eat me rather than protect me.'

Tony contained a sigh of relief as the horrific image of Aidan roaming all over the countryside with a fully grown tiger had flashed in front of her eyes. 'Yes I think a dog is much less likely to think of you as a tasty snack than a tiger.'

The carriage drew up at the church while Andre held his sides as he laughed in delight at the interchange between the adorable siblings.

What A Princess You Would Make

Jumping out of the coach, Andre became more serious as he insisted that they wait inside the vehicle while he made certain that it was safe to enter the church. Having been raised a good Catholic boy, Andre felt a touch nervous entering any temple of God wearing both of Caleb's gun holsters concealed under his jacket. The church was empty except for Louise, François, the Reverend Matthew Gray and his wife Heather.

When the church roof didn't miraculously fall down on his head, Andre sighed in relief. *I hope that God will forgive me as I'm taking the protection of the betrothed couple very, very seriously.* Sighting Andre as he cast a searching glance around the church, Matthew Gray came sailing down the centre aisle, already attired in his ceremonial robes.

'Bring them into the vestry, Monsieur Guillaume. They can wait there while we get everyone seated.'

"Right you are Father.' Andre slipped outside again to shepherd his charges inside.

There was a low fire burning in the vestry which meant that the room was toasty warm but being once again in the vestry of a church brought memories flooding back of seeking sanctuary in another church not that long ago in Hon Fleur. Trembling slightly, although the fire was inviting, Aidan clung possessively to his future brother as Tony carefully un-bandaged Caleb's eyes. Sliding the dark lens glasses on once more, Caleb glanced down at the scared little boy.

'Would you rather we wait in the church Aidan? Then you can tell me the names of all the people as they enter the church.'

Isabella was touched by her son's kindness and understanding of the boy's fears. 'It is much warmer in here but of you want to sit in the church I think I saw Mary with your fur rug Aidan,' added Isabella.

The younger Lord shook his head. 'No thank you Ma'am. I'll stay here with Tony and Caleb. With them I am safe!' Aidan spoke these last words a little more firmly, perhaps to convince himself more so that anyone else.

'Well I'll leave Monsieur Guillaume on guard duty while I see what I can do to help get everyone seated.' Isabella kissed her son's cheek before she slipped out of the room.

Moving to sit down in an arm chair beside the fireplace, Caleb settled Aidan comfortably on his lap before raising his eyes to rest upon Tony. Slowly he scanned her from head to toe. Tony didn't realise that she had been holding her breath until Caleb smiled his approval and she let her breath out in a sigh.

'Your father was right, my beautiful elfling. What a princess you would make.'

Tony caught back a sob as she dropped down to her knees beside Caleb's chair. 'Only if you are my prince!' Caressing her hand against his cheek, she passionately kissed him. Tenderly he brushed his thumb against her cheek to sweep away a tear.

'Don't cry Tony. Were you really worried what I'd think about your dress?'

Uttering a watery chuckle, she pulled a handkerchief from the sleeve of her dress and dabbed her eyes. 'I was starting to think that I may have been childish or extravagant when I chose this dress. I thought you might say I was being ridiculous.'

Smiling kindly, he helped Tony to her feet and into the chair opposite him.

'Not at all, it suits you perfectly. Besides which when Andre showed me what he wanted me to wear, I had an inkling as to what was ahead of me.'

Stiffening in indignation, Tony cast a hurt look at her beloved. 'So were you just placating me about how you really feel about my choice of dress?'

Andre groaned in disbelief as he couldn't believe that Caleb had walked straight into that rebuke.

'No tigress, put your claws away. I just meant it wasn't a total surprise to me, not that it was an unpleasant surprise.' A slow sexy smile appeared on Caleb's face, taking Tony's breath away as his eyes twinkled wickedly. 'Actually I can think of several scenarios where we can utilise that dress. Several fairy tales spring to mind. Both Snow White and Sleeping Beauty needed to be awoken with a kiss from their handsome prince.' His smile widened. 'Then there is Rapunzel in her ivory tower waiting for her prince to rescue her.'

Tony struggled to breathe, she certainly was unable to speak, so caught up by the sexy, sultry tone of Caleb's voice. The imagery was so evocative, so filled with passionate potential that she felt a blush sweep across her face and enflame her blood with heat and longing. Andre felt like he was intruding upon something very personal, ultimately intimate but even before he could take a step towards the door to give the engaged couple some privacy, Aidan broke the spell.

Glancing critically from one to the other, Aidan said, 'But when did Tony ever sit idly by waiting for some man to rescue her? Is that really the kind of woman you want big brother? Or is this just naughty make believe?'

Tousling Aidan's hair, Caleb laughed. He had been so swept up in creating the evocative imagery with Tony that he had momentarily forgotten that anyone else was present. 'Naughty make believe is correct. I don't think that any of us would be alive today if Tony was a helpless, meek and timid princess. It is important, though, for a man's ego for him to be the master occasionally.' He raised laughing eyes to meet Tony's and she had to force down a giggle as Aidan's tiny brows had puckered into a frown.

'Everything is going to change now isn't it?' There was incredible sadness in his voice. Like his sister, he felt that change can be frightening and not always a good thing. Reaching out to take Aidan's hands, Tony looked him squarely in his eyes.

'Some things will change Little Bear, but not everything. Soon I'll be leaving the Manor to make a life with Caleb but we will never be far from you. Duncan will be leaving for London and in a few months you'll have a new little brother or sister. That doesn't mean that I'll stop loving you or that Caleb won't want to spend time with his Little Bear.'

'There will come a time when you'd rather be playing with your friends from school than with us and that is a change that we will have to accept. It won't mean that you love us any less but that you need us a little less as a part of your growing up.'

Aidan sniffed inelegantly. 'What if these friends and I are bored, can I still bring them over to Delacourt Hall so we find something to do?'

'I'd like that very much Aidan.' Tony used her handkerchief to wipe her brother's eyes and urged him to blow his nose. Gazing lovingly at Tony, Caleb felt his heart was so full that it hurt.

'You're going to make one sensational mother!' He rose out of his chair and with Aidan in his arms, held out his hand towards Tony.

Smiling wistfully as she linked her arm through his, she said, 'Remind me of this conversation when it comes time for me to allow Aidan to draw away as he grows up.'

Tenderly kissing her cheek, Caleb chuckled, 'When that time does come, I think you'll have your hands full with our own children.'

'Is that a promise, my Lord?' Tony's voice was a little unsteady as the thought of the future where Aidan wouldn't need her any more had hurt.

Caleb's eyes twinkled wickedly. 'We'll just have to keep practicing until we have as many little bundles of joy that your heart desires.'

Rolling his eyes, Aidan glanced across at an amused Andre. 'They're being naughty again aren't they Monsieur Guillaume?'

Laughing, Andre agreed. *I am really going to miss this engaging family when I eventually return to France.* Opening the door to check if it was time for the lovers to be wed, Andre hoped, *that they don't change their minds about putting their story on paper as it is gold.*

My Little Tom Boy

Trying to not look as disenchanted as he felt, the Earl put his wife's foibles to the back of his mind. He collared Caleb as he stepped out of the vestry following Andre.

'We're nearly ready, my boy, but the Moreau brothers and Juliette Martin have just arrived and I thought you'd want to have a brief word with them before the ceremony starts.'

'Of course my Lord,' as he held out his hand to Aidan, the Earl managed to school his expression as his son refused to leave Caleb's arms. 'I want to finally lay eyes on François too now that my bandages have been removed,' Caleb added, accepting from the Earl, Aidan's fur rug and wrapping it round the boy.

Sympathetically, the Earl patted his shoulder, 'No matter how beautiful he is, remember that it's you Tony wants to marry. No question about that!'

Caleb cast him a speaking glance. 'Thank you for boosting my confidence, my Lord!' he drawled.

The Earl's face relaxed into a grin. 'Sorry and its time you called me "Julius" unless you feel comfortable calling me "father".'

When Caleb looked at him absolutely stunned, Earl Stirling added, 'I'm not trying to replace your father, Caleb, but we are going to be family.'

'Thank you Sir. I'll consider it. Excuse me.'

As Caleb and Aidan headed over to greet their French visitors, the Earl stepped inside the vestry. 'I've frightened him, haven't I?' He asked Tony and Andre, who had stayed to protect the bride.

'It has been a lot to take in within a very short period of time, Lord Stirling,' soothed Andre. 'Caleb is still very much in protective mode and probably can't process anything else right now.'

'Oh!' There was a pause as the Earl considered what the French Author had said. 'Do you think that there is still something to be protective about?'

Casting a swift glance across at Tony, Andre didn't want to frighten her on her big day but he spoke honestly. 'I don't think we're quite finished yet, my Lord. If you'll excuse me, I'll just check up on Caleb and Aidan.' Andre bowed to the Earl but placed a tender kiss against Tony's cheek. 'I would like to paint you just like this... a vision of beauty, Innocence and yet regal!' The Frenchman kissed her other cheek before leaving the room.

For a moment the Earl stared at the closed door before turning his eyes to study his daughter.

'He's right, my little tomboy has become a very beautiful young Lady. I must find a painter before the blushing bride becomes a glowing mother.'

Tony's eyebrows rose in surprise. 'Before I become fat and ugly?' She teased.

'No, no! I want a portrait of you then as well but I want the painter to capture you on canvas just as you are now.' The Earl raised a slightly trembling hand to caress his daughter's cheek. 'So like your mother. I wish…' He swallowed hard on the lump constricting his throat. 'I hope Caleb knows just how lucky he truly is.'

Taking her father's hand in hers, she smiled mischievously. 'You don't think I'll drive him crazy?'

The Earl chuckled. 'You're bound to, baby girl but that is half the fun of being with your soul mate; you'll enjoy that journey into madness together. The only way I'll be any happier for you than at this moment, is when you present me with my first grandchild.'

Kissing Tony's cheek, the Earl was surprised when she threw her arms around him as she tried to contain a sob.

'Thank you Papa.'

'Now, now, no tears baby girl. You don't want the groom to think you're unhappy to marry him,' teased the Earl as he brushed away a stray tear that fell down her cheek. Accepting her father's handkerchief, Tony managed to compose herself again.

I can't believe how emotional I am acting. Is it normal for brides to cry at their own wedding? Or is this just reaction to all that we have been through the past twelve days? Such was the state of her nerves that she jumped when the door to the vestry was unceremoniously thrown open and her cousin Patrick entered the room.

Nice To Finally See You

It wasn't in the least difficult for Caleb to locate his French visitors. Seven men and three women stood out as distinctly French. Scanning the group as he strode down the aisle, Caleb tried to sort out who was who. He had already seen Rosemary and could identify a definite family resemblance amongst five of the men so Caleb assured that they were therefore Rosemary's brothers. The older of the other two gentlemen stepped forward to embrace Caleb and Aidan kissing the groom on each cheek before standing back to scan Caleb's features.

'So you have your eyesight back cousin? Bon! Now I know you have already been introduced to everyone but I'll just put a face to the voice you may remember,' said Phillippe Du Bois. Putting his arm around Caleb, he led him towards the group of people who were standing a little nervous, halfway down the middle aisle.

'Thank you Phillippe. I'm surprised you managed to get away from Paris. I thought you'd have funeral commitments.'

Phillippe gestured to where Lady Margarette was warmly embracing a French version of herself, Phillippe's mother, Monique Du Bois.

'Maman insisted that we made the journey, besides,' Phillippe chuckled, 'Maman was getting sick of the pomp and ceremony and wanted something happy to celebrate for a change.'

Keeping a tight grasp upon Aidan, Caleb cast a quick searching look over the boy. 'Are you warm enough Aidan?' The fur rug was loosely draped around Aidan but as the church was a tad cooler than the vestry, the boy now drew it tighter around him.

'I'm all right.' The little Lord's eyes lit up as he called out, 'Nanny!' and held out his hands to Louise. Smiling, Louise took Aidan's hands into her own but raised questioning eyes to Caleb.

'Is it all right, my Lord?'

Smiling, Caleb immediately handed Aidan across to her. 'Of course, you don't want us dead now do you?' He teased but there was a touch of pain in those words.

Turning to Juliette Martin, Caleb bowed elegantly over her hand and only just managed to remember he didn't need to speak in French any more. 'Madame Martin we're honoured that you could join us. Tony has been worried about the damage done to your hotel - what with the fire and an angry mob.'

Juliette smiled. 'It was mostly smoke to force everyone out, as for the mob, well the Moreau boys returned to Paris from Dieppe in the mood for a fight. Apparently there was less of a dust up rescuing you than they had anticipated.'

'I was extremely grateful for their timely arrival. Tell me who is whom?' Spying the effeminate beauty of one man, Caleb added, 'this is obviously Theodore.'

Nodding, as she linked her arm through Caleb's, Juliette re-introduced him to Emile, Bruno, Isaac and Gilbert. When Caleb paused at the only gentleman not introduced, he choked and his heart was squeezed remorselessly beneath his ribs. Standing in front of him was a god, a slightly black and blue god, but a god none the less.

'My God! François? You are every woman's dream!' moaned Caleb, so overcome by the vision of masculine splendour that he didn't resist as François cupped Caleb's face between his gentle hands and kissed him on both cheeks.

Into Caleb's ear, François whispered, 'You're not so bad yourself, my Lord. Shall I tell you what I'd like to do with such a magnificent specimen of masculinity that stands before me?'

Blushing Caleb drew back. 'Thank you but no.' Still doubtful, he scanned the young Frenchman's chiselled features.

'It is you Tony loves and wants to be loved by. Have faith in your own qualities and stop being so humble!' François stepped back and Caleb was forced to see himself in a new light.

As Andre joined the reunion and assisted in finding seats for the visitors, Caleb noted the late arrival of Patrick Stirling. Instinctively his hand reached for his gun holsters but fell upon his broad sword instead. Caleb cast a quick glance around to locate Aidan. The boy was safe enough seated on Nanny's knee so Caleb's eyes followed Patrick's movements down the side aisle as he headed for the vestry.

Meeting Andre's eyes, Caleb silently directed his attention towards Patrick as he threw open the vestry door. Andre noted that Caleb's hand tightened upon his sword and held up his own hand for Caleb to stay there while he checked on Tony and the Earl. It took a concentrated effort but Caleb nodded and holding out his arms to Aidan, allowed Andre to trot after Patrick.

Scooping the boy up, Caleb joined his cousin Geoff and the Reverend Gray at the altar. *Not that I don't fully trust any of our French visitors to look after Aidan but until I know that Tony is all right, I am going to keep Aidan glued to my side.*

Am I too late?

'Thank Goodness, I'm not too late!" Patrick started talking the moment he entered the vestry and seemed oblivious as the Earl protectively drew his daughter behind him.

'Too late for what Patrick?' asked Tony. 'To stop the wedding?'

A little startled Patrick halted in his tracks and glanced from his uncle to his cousin. 'Not at all! Too late to warn you that you and Lord Delacourt could still be in terrible danger.' Patrick paused as if for dramatic effect but as Tony had been through so much the past fortnight she was unmoved by her cousin's dire warning.

The Earl was equally unimpressed. 'Get on with it Patrick. Did you learn something in London?'

Managing to conceal his disappointment at their lack of appreciation for his art of dramatic deliverance, Patrick said, 'London seems very well informed with Tony's adventure abroad and the Ton can talk of nothing else! The press seems to be getting their information directly from within Stirling Manor!'

The Earl was a little dismissive of Patrick's news. 'Noah, the Groom in league with an ex-Footman Adam? They have been taken care of. Anything else?'

Set on the back foot, Patrick was momentarily stunned as he had thought he was delivering ground breaking news. His eyes closed to slits as he dealt his final card. 'Before leaving London, I dropped in on Agnes Henry to check upon her. She wasn't home.'

Raising his hand to stroke his chin, the Earl paused as he thought through what Patrick meant.

'Not at home to visitors or not at home at all?' the Earl asked.

Containing a grin, Patrick knew that he had finally hooked his uncle's interest. 'Not at all! She had left London at first light. You heard her swear vengeance against Lord Delacourt which means that Tony is also in danger.'

'Damn it!' The Earl didn't get any further as Andre entered the room. Looking sharply from each of their faces, Andre said, 'What is it? Has something happened? How can I help?'

Tony was impressed by Andre's calm, no nonsense tone. 'Agnes Henry has vowed revenge on Caleb for killing her son and she is no longer in London.' She summarised the situation succinctly and without Patrick's dramatic emphasis.

Nodding, Andre was already out of the door again as he said, 'Don't worry, I'm on it!' He grabbed Patrick by the collar and dragged him out of the vestry with him.

Protecting Their Own!

Turning as Andre approached, Caleb's eyebrows rose in query at the earnest look on the Frenchman's face.

'Problem?'

Andre nodded. 'Agnes Henry is no longer in London.' He looked across at Reverend Gray. 'Are the front double doors the only way into the church, Father?'

Matthew Gray shook his head. 'There is access via the vestry but I always keep the outer door locked.' He had no idea that trouble could descend upon his little church.

'Good,' Andre was already moving away when he said, 'don't worry Caleb! I've got this!' Striding down the church aisle, Andre halted beside Phillippe Du Bois and the Moreau brothers. Standing beside Caleb, Patrick watched as the men immediately rose out of their seats and followed Andre's brief instructions.

Two men moved to the corner of the back pew, two more took up the same position on the other side of the church, two came up to sit in the front pew closest to the vestry and another man joined Andre on the front pew on the opposite side of the altar.

'What are they doing?' asked Patrick.

Caleb smiled grimly. 'Protecting their own!' Glancing across at Reverend Gray, he added, 'Are we ready to do this?'

Bemused, Matthew nodded and Patrick went back to the vestry to inform the Earl before finding a seat.

As Tony entered the church upon her father's arm, the whole congregation rose to their feet. There were murmurs of appreciation and surprise at the sight of this medieval princess as she glided towards the altar and her prince. When they had reached Caleb's side, Matthew cleared his throat.

'Who so giveth this woman away?'

The Earl smiled fondly at his daughter. 'I do,' tenderly kissing Tony's cheek, he then reached out to take Aidan's hand from Caleb's before taking a seat beside Charlotte; Geoff stood beside Caleb and Rosemary and Mary joined Tony. Mary took the roses bouquet so that Tony could take Caleb's hands as Matthew Gray began the ceremony.

There was absolute silence when Matthew reached the part asking the congregation if anyone had a reason this couple should not be married; one or two eyes travelled to rest upon Patrick and Rosemary cast an uncertain glance across at Andre but he seemed to be more interested in looking back at the main doors.

With no objections raised, Caleb and Tony were allowed to exchange their vows. As he slipped a wedding ring onto Tony's finger, she raised her eyes to meet his and a single tear ran down her cheek. *This is finally, really happening and nothing is going to come between us.*

When Matthew said, 'You may now kiss your bride.' The congregation rose to their feet and cheered as Caleb tenderly cupped Tony's face and briefly kissed her. There was a signing of the official documents and finally, Tony and Caleb turned to those assembled as Lord and Lady Delacourt. Slipping out of his father's hold, Aidan jumped into Caleb's arms.

'Now I have a big brother and a big sister!' He cried out in glee.

Where Are My Brothers?

The double doors flew open, with such violence that they slammed back against the wall with an echoing bang. Five heavily armed men strode into the church and the leader fired a warning shot into the ceiling. There were screams of terror as nearly all the congregation hid behind their pews. The Moreau brothers remained standing as did Phillippe, Andre and François.

What surprised Tony was that they each carried at least one if not two pistols. Caleb calmly handed Aidan to Tony and drew her behind him as he placed his hand onto the hilt of his sword. Geoff remained standing beside his cousin in front of the altar as did the Earl.

'Where are my brothers?' The leader demanded, pointing a pistol at Earl Stirling.

'As I have no idea who you are, I therefore have no idea where your kin may be,' drawled the Earl. Casting a quick scrutinising glance over the leader and noting that he had a slight burn mark on the side of his face where it had come so very close to the hobs of an Aga stove, Caleb realised his identity.

'Peter Doyle and a couple of mates who had been drinking in the Stirling Arms the night Nigel Sutherland first confronted Tony.' Caleb explained.

'Where are Adam and Noah?' Peter demanded.

'Gone,' said the Earl, 'The Bow Street Runner took them up to London as soon as it was light.'

'Then it is up to us to avenge the wrong you made against Adam!' Peter took a step forward but for the first time, noticed the Frenchmen standing in front of him and his own brothers. Men who also aimed various weapons in his direction.

I wouldn't do that if I were you, Doyle,' said Caleb, 'lay down your weapons and accept whatever penalty the authorities bestow upon you.'

'Or what?' Peter spat out.

One of Caleb's eyebrows rose slowly, 'Or you may join Adam in the London morgue.'

'Oh no!' The cry of dismay came from Mary as she crouched behind a pew, attempting to protect Rosemary. 'So I did kill him?'

The Earl turned to cast the Maid an apologetic look. 'Sorry Mary, I was going to tell you tomorrow. I didn't want to spoil today's celebration.'

Peter roared. 'Then I'll kill her first and then you Lord Stirling for abandoning Adam when he was caught stealing for you!'

The Earl placed himself in front of Mary. 'How many times do I have to say that Adam was not stealing alcohol for me? He just wouldn't admit that he had a serious drinking problem!'

'Liar!' spat out Peter.

'No, he's not lying Pete,' said a voice from behind Peter Doyle and caused the leader to spin around in disbelief.

'Noah? But he said you were in London.'

The Groom nodded to Officer Bell standing beside him, and the other armed officers of the law who were entering the church behind him.

'I convinced Officer Bell that I might be able to stop you doing something idiotic and maybe getting yourself killed. Adam lied to us Pete.' The Groom held his hand out towards his brother.

'He wouldn't! Not after Pa…'

Noah shook his head. 'I was with Adam when he died. He admitted it at the end. He was an alcoholic just like Pa.'

Officer Bell spoke softly and encouragingly, 'Hand over your weapons son and it'll go better for you in court. You haven't hurt anyone yet, why don't we keep it that way? These people didn't force the demon drink upon your brother, let's go outside and have a little chat. Hum? Let these people enjoy their special day in peace.'

As the Bow Street Runner took a step closer to the armed intruders, Peter Doyle folded. Biting back a sob he handed his pistols to Officer Bell. A sigh of relief swept through the congregation as the Doyle clan followed Peter's lead and disarmed before they were all calmly led out of the church.

Get Them Out Of Here!

Noise erupted inside the church as everyone began to speak at once and the Earl turned to grasp Mary firmly by the hand. 'Take my children into the vestry, all this fuss and noise will be too much for them. Once Bell has taken away the Doyle family it'll be safe to head back home.' He gave her a gentle push towards Tony as he set about the task of soothing his wife who was having hysterics.

Mary took Caleb and Tony by the arm and led them away from the noise that echoed throughout the church. Andre wished, *I could escape with them but I need to stand down my own private troops and assist where needed as Charlotte is not the only female overcome by the shock of being held up... in a church... at a wedding.*

Taking Aidan out of Tony's arms, Mary popped him down in front of the vestry fireplace and poured him a drink. She was a little surprised at his calm acceptance showing that such violence had not upset the young Lord. Glancing up Aidan smiled and nodded his head towards where Caleb had taken Tony into his arms.

'I have a big brother and a big sister to protect me.' The boy explained.

Exhaling slowly, Mary found that she was shaking slightly in shock and didn't raise a protest as Tony turned and wrapped her arms around her Maid.

'Are you sure it isn't going to be like this every day my Lady?' Mary felt her tremor subside with Tony's hug. Her question caused Caleb to chuckle as he laid his hand under Mary's elbow and extracting her from Tony's arms, led Mary to sit down.

'I certainly hope not,' he said, 'the only excitement I want for the next few months is Aidan visiting us and myself finding pleasure with my wife.'

Blushing, Tony would have protested but his last two words distracted her. 'Oh! I like the sound of that – your wife! We're really married now aren't we? I'm not dreaming?' She reached up to caress Caleb's cheek.

His smile lit up the room. 'Then we're both having the same dream, my elfling.' Caleb lowered his head to kiss his bride but the recent events meant that his warrior instinct was still running high. So when the door opened, he instinctively reached for his sword.

Earl Stirling raised his hands submissively. 'Hold on there, my boy, it's not the done thing to murder your father-in–law on your wedding day.' He closed the door behind him, cutting out the noise in the church.

'Sorry sir,' Caleb removed his hand from the hilt of his sword.

'I've arranged for your carriage to be brought round to the vestry door. It's going to take some time for us to calm down out there and I'd rather you get Aidan home again. Get warm, have a little rest and then we can all celebrate your wedding together. So Tony re-bandage Caleb's burns and Mary go with them.' The Earl pressed a pistol into the Maid's hand that he had liberated from Andre.

'Surely I'd be more use to you calming the sensitive ladies?'

The Earl shook his head. 'No, I'd rather you protect my children.' Pausing to kiss Tony's cheek, the Earl added, 'We won't be too far behind you. The shock is starting to wear off.' Taking a deep breath, the Earl left the sanctuary of the vestry and stepped back out into the subsiding noise.

While they waited for the carriage, Tony sat Caleb down to re-bandage his burns and eyes. *I am a little reluctant to return to darkness right now we might still be in danger,* but Caleb relaxed as Mary pressed into his hand the pistol given to her by the Earl. *Not being used to handling a broad sword, I cannot seriously think of it as a weapon but I feel more confident with a gun in my possession.*

Mary unlocked the outer vestry door and glanced cautiously around outside before she signalled that it was safe for her charges to alight into the carriage which had just pulled up alongside the open door. Tony picked up Aidan and laid her free hand on Caleb's arm to lead him around the furniture.

As the carriage door closed behind them and they drew away from the church, they were finally married. Tony sighed in relief, *We had avoided any bloodshed and we are surrounded by the people who matter the most – our family and friends.*

Home Safe

When Preston opened the front doors at the Manor, he was unable to control his surprise that only one carriage had drawn up at the door step. Stepping forward to assist the bride and groom out of their vehicle he spoke a little hastier than normal.

'What has happened Lady Tony? Did anything stop you getting married?'

Tony received Aidan from Mary before the Maid disembarked.

'No, we're married Preston. Papa and our other guests will be along as soon as possible. I must take Aidan upstairs to get warm and remove Caleb's bandages.'

Surprising her, Preston took Aidan out of her arms. 'I need to discuss something with you and Lord Caleb.'

Pausing only for a moment, Tony finally nodded. 'Of course Preston. Are you unwell? You look a little shaken.'

Preston followed them inside and up the main staircase. 'I'd rather explain myself in his Lordship's room. You'd better come too Mary.' The Butler gestured for the Maid to fall in behind him as Tony linked her arm through Caleb's for stability up the stairs.

Why Are We Waiting?

By the time the Earl, the rest of the family, the other guests and locals arrived at the Manor, Preston was once again awaiting them in the entrance hall. Having heard of the Doyle brothers attack on the wedding ceremony, Preston had brought up from the cellar several bottles of brandy just in case it was required if anyone was still suffering from shock. The guests and local people were shepherded into the ball room where Mrs Hill had already begun filling tables with delicious finger food.

The family were led into the drawing room so that they could recover before they joined the happy couple and their guests. Lizzy thought that it was perhaps prudent to take her sister Charlotte up to her own room to lie down as the shock had traumatised the young Countess. The Earl refused to meet the obvious question in the raised eyebrow of his mother as the Dowager Countess had no patience for vapourish women.

Half an hour passed. An hour passed and still there was no appearance of Tony, Caleb and Aidan. Checking his fob watch, the Earl finally pulled the bell to summon Preston. When the Butler promptly appeared, the Earl said, 'It is time the newlyweds came down Preston. If Aidan isn't up to leaving the room, an armed servant can be left to guard him,' Earl Stirling stated quietly, not wishing to intrude on the new freedom the lovers now had to be able to give into their passionate desires but reminding them they had a duty to fulfil first.

'Yes my Lord. At once.' Preston had just opened the drawing room door to depart when everyone in the room heard a crash of a metal tray and a horrific scream. Geoff and Patrick leapt to their feet but the Earl also rising, held out his hand to halt them.

'Stay here and protect the ladies. I'll call you if I need you.' Earl Stirling strode out of the room followed closely by Preston. In the spacious entrance hall they were met by Andre, Phillippe and Doctor Masters.

'What on earth has befallen us now?' asked the bemused Doctor.

The Earl laid a hand on Phillippe's shoulder, 'Have the Moreau brothers stand guard over the guests in the ballroom. Doctor come with us, we may need your services.' As Phillippe returned to the ballroom, the others followed the Earl smartly up the stairs.

I Failed Them!

Out of Caleb's room, Mary ran in a blind panic. She was as white as a sheet, her eyes open wide in horror and she was trembling violently. Seeing the four men moving swiftly towards her, Mary flung herself at the Earl, grasping his jacket lapels and almost collapsing into his arms.

'Steady on Mary, a spilt tray of drinks isn't worth all these histrionics.' The Earl found himself almost completely supporting the trembling Maid.

'I thought... they were sleeping... but then I saw... their lips are blue... their faces grey... they're not breathing! I have failed to protect them!' As Mary burst into tears, the Earl thrust her into the Doctor's arms and threw open the bedroom door. Swallowing hard on the lump in his throat trying to choke him, Earl Stirling was oblivious to the fact that the others followed him into the room.

Lying together on the bed, still in their wedding costumes except for Caleb removing his broad sword, they could have just been asleep. Aidan lay curled up between the two adults and his arms were wrapped around his sister. Closing his eyes, the Earl took a deep, shuddering breath and slowly opened his eyes again but all the wishing wasn't going to make it happen.

Mary had described them perfectly. Their faces were now grey, their lips had a blue tinge and most importantly, they weren't breathing. When the Earl's legs began to collapse beneath him, Andre was at his elbow, supporting him across to one of the arm chairs. Into the other chair Doctor Masters had already placed a weeping Mary.

Quietly closing the bedroom door, Preston cleared his throat. 'Monsieur Guillaume, I believe Officer Bell is here to take statements about what occurred in church. Could you ask him to join us please? Not a word to anyone about this just yet. It will be his Lordship's duty to inform the family first of this tragic turn of events.'

Andre nodded. 'Of course. I think Lord Stirling could do with something to drink. Shall I bring up some brandy?'

The Earl shuddered. 'Perhaps just a glass of cordial.' He gestured vaguely towards the jugs situated on the desk.

'No!' The Doctor's firmness surprised them all. 'They haven't been shot, this looks like poison! Nothing should be consumed from within this room until I have tested it.'

Preston pulled himself together. 'I'll have everything bottled up so that you can take it away and test the contents. This chocolate pot feels hot.' The Butler lowered his gaze to Mary.

'I'd only just brought it in before collecting the glasses of champagne on a tray left outside in the hall way. Oh Lord Stirling! I've ruined a pair of your good crystal glasses!'

The Earl shook his head. 'It doesn't matter Mary. Nothing matters now. My darling children gone!'

As the Earl buried his head into his hands Preston laid his hand on Mary's shoulder. 'Take the jugs downstairs and place the contents into jars for the Doctor.'

Glancing up at Doctor Masters, Preston asked, 'Is it all right to then wash the jugs and glasses or must we wait for Officer Bell to see them in situ.'

'The contents is all we need,' said the Doctor.

Andre assisted Mary as she rose and picked up the tray of cordial jugs and he quietly closed the door behind their departure. The Author offered to escort Mary down to the servants' domain but she insisted that he needed to find Abraham Bell immediately.

Running down the stairs Andre's heart was pounding painfully in his chest. *This is not the ending that I had foreseen for the brave masqueraders. Perhaps I truly am more like Rosemary than I had previously admitted, I had wanted the romantic fairy tale ending of living happily ever after. What have we missed? Who have we overlooked as a suspect?*

Grabbing Officer Bell, a bottle of brandy and half a dozen glasses, Andre led the way back up to the nightmare. *Only a handful of people know of the horror, but soon the Earl will have to turn the celebration of life into a mourning of death. The outpouring of grief, shock and disbelief is going to be monumental and to deal with that; a little fortification is in order.*

They're All Dead!

When the time came, Andre descended to the ground floor with the Earl and Preston. Doctor Masters and Officer Bell took the jars Mary supplied of the cordials from the bedroom and headed off to the Doctor's surgery to test which poison had been used to murder Caleb, Tony and Aidan. Mary remained in Caleb's room to stop anyone accidently wandering in or interfering with their bodies.

Dragging in a deep breath, Earl Stirling paused, momentarily preparing himself for his family's reaction before he finally allowed Preston to open the door to the drawing room.

Glancing around from the half attention she had bestowed on Patience Sinclair's speculation about the colourful future ahead of the newlyweds, Lady Margarette took one look at her son's drawn features and stiffened. 'What is it Julius? Has someone cut themselves dropping a tray of glasses?' demanded the Dowager and all talk in the room immediately creased as attention became focused on the Earl.

'It's worse than that mother; Mary dropped a tray with champagne glasses and screamed when she entered Caleb's room and...' That lump was back trying to choke the words that uttering them aloud would mean that they were real.

Geoff uttered a wicked laugh. 'They couldn't wait to consummate their marriage? Well any of us could have predicted that!'

Swallowing hard, the Earl managed to shake his head. 'No Geoff, Caleb and Tony weren't making love… they… they're all dead!'

A deafening silence followed the Earl's revelation as it seemed impossible, improbable to comprehend.

'No! No! No!' Isabella chanted in disbelief as she rose to her feet. 'I… I want to see my son! I want to see my new daughter!' Her voice caught as reality began to sink in and tears streamed down her face.

'No it's not advisable Isabella. You don't want to remember them that way.' The Earl was firm but tried to protect her from the full horror. Geoff put his arm supportively around his aunt's shoulders.

'Why?' He asked. 'How did they die? Why didn't anyone hear any gun shots?' The bluntness of his questions caused Patience to turn sobbing into her husband's arms.

'No, they weren't shot; they were poisoned,' admitted the Earl.

Those assembled gasped and looked at the refreshments they had been consuming since their return from the church. Preston hastened to reassure their horrified thoughts.

'The wine I brought up after Lady Tony told me what had happened at the church. There's been a servant at all times in the ballroom and Mrs Hill and several of her girls have been in the kitchen so no food or drink downstairs can have been tainted.' The Butler lost his normal cool facade. 'It's my fault. I never thought that we needed to keep guard over the rooms upstairs if the downstairs doors were covered.'

Snapping his fingers, Patrick said, 'Agnes Henry! She wanted her revenge on Caleb for the death of Claude!'

The Earl shook his head. 'But to kill Tony and Aidan as well? Would Agnes risk losing a Henry heir to the title?'

Stroking his chin as he paced up and down the room, Patrick stated, 'She isn't in her right mind, uncle. Her beloved son has been taken from her so Agnes isn't thinking straight. She may be banking on the fact that with Charlotte in the family way again she'll produce another son.'

'Oh!' That sad, forlorn sound came from Preston. 'The Pattersons had arrived to offer their services as protection when a servant came running to find me. He had seen a woman running away from the house. He'd never seen Mrs Henry before but his description brought her to my mind. Solitaire, sorry Mr Patterson said that they'd go after her. I… I haven't seen them since.'

The Dowager Countess rose slowly, regally to her feet. 'You can discuss possible suspects later Julius. You need to inform the staff and then our guests waiting in the ballroom. I recommend that you don't tell Charlotte just yet. Wait until her nerves have recovered from this morning's ordeal. I shall be in my room if you need me.'

Ever the perfect Butler, Preston offered his arm to Lady Margarette and as he escorted her out of the room, those left inside heard her ask, 'I'm sure that you will have already considered the need to change the jugs in all the bedrooms, Preston. Just to be on the safe side.'

'Yes my Lady.'

The other ladies followed the Dowager's example and retired to their rooms as Earl Stirling had to impart the terrible news two more times. The Manor could not have been cleared any quicker even if the Earl had declared the house riddled with small pox.

There were of course exceptions. François led a weeping Louise up to her room, Phillippe took his mother Monique up to Lady Margarette's room so that the sisters could grieve together.

Reverend Matthew Gray and his wife, Heather, refused to leave until they had offered any support the family might need.

Juliette Martin and the Moreau brothers had intended to return home the next morning but wondered if they should depart now so the Stirling family weren't inundated with guests. The Earl thanked them for their thoughtfulness but Officer Bell didn't want anyone leaving the district until he had narrowed down his list of suspects. Not that the Earl thought, nor did the Bow Street Runner think that their French visitors had anything to do with this murder.

Rosemary insisted that Mary shouldn't be left alone after such a horrific shock but the Earl stated that Mary was in fact keeping vigil in Caleb's room. Looking a little mulish, Rosemary insisted that was even more reason the devoted Maid should have someone with her. The besieged Earl glanced imploringly at Andre but after careful consideration the Author actually agreed with Rosemary.

Sighing the Earl waved them up the stairs with his permission and rubbing a slightly unsteady hand across his brow, Earl Stirling contemplated what he needed to do next. *With a throbbing head, a heavy heart and a grief that is trying to physically tear me apart, I am surprised that my stomach actually has the audacity to indicate it is hungry.* He had been about to ascend the stairs to check on Charlotte but realising that his features would too readily betray his grief, the Earl wandered back into the ballroom.

Mrs Hill was selecting what was more suitable for a bereavement luncheon while Stewards and Kitchen Maids packed up baskets of food that would then be distributed throughout the families in the village and his Lordship's tenement. With the appearance of the Earl, the servants halted activity and curtsied or bowed expecting to have to leave their task.

The Earl waved them on to continue as he absently moved down the table, seeing the food before him as he sampled this and that but not really knowing what he put into his mouth or what it tasted like. It was a mechanical action to satisfy one emptiness inside of him, while another emptiness could never be filled.

Taking pity on the Earl and how he made it difficult for her staff to continue to work, Mrs Hill loaded up a plate of what she knew to be the Earl's favourite foods and gently persuaded him to retire to his library as Preston was supervising the laying of the table in the dining room for luncheon.

Considering Suspects

Lord Stirling was just finishing up with some cheese and was wondering, *Why does the cheese, in fact nearly all the produce, produced from our own farm seem to taste better than any other?* When Preston announced several visitors at once, Doctor Masters entered with Officer Bell and, a reluctant to report, Solitaire. Sighing as he threw himself into a chair, the Doctor said bluntly, 'Cyanide!' Wincing, the Earl glanced across at the standing Bell who confirmed their findings.

'I'm afraid so, my Lord. All three jugs had been tampered with.' Turning as Preston was about to depart, Bell stopped him. 'Please stay Mr Preston. We need to discuss who may have had access to the upstairs rooms this morning.'

Bowing his head, Preston quietly closed the door as he came back into the library. Pushing his plate away from him, the Earl looked a little puzzled.

'Do you have any reason to believe it can be anyone other than my mother-in-law?'

A grim smile appeared on Bell's face. 'I don't want to be blindsided by so obvious a suspect, my Lord. I want to consider all possible options first.'

'So where do you want to start?' The Earl had never before sounded so business like.

Officer Bell gestured towards the desk. 'Do you mind if I borrow your desk my Lord?' Hearing the slight gasp from Preston, Bell hastened to reassure. 'I don't mean Lord Stirling's seat but a corner of the desk so that I can write down all the suspects and their motives or opportunities to commit murder.'

The Earl wasn't at all offended but had already risen from his seat. 'Sit. There are paper, quills, ink or pencils if you prefer. I'm relying on you to find out who murdered my children Mr Bell. This should have been the happiest day in their young lives and not...' The Earl broke off as the raw emotions choked him.

Bell placed his hand upon Earl Stirling's arm. 'We will sort this out my Lord, once the suspects have been reduced to a more manageable list. We need to look at everyone's motives, opportunities and means, everyone who had had access to this house, to begin with, is a suspect.'

Dragging in a deep, steadying breath, the Earl nodded. 'No exceptions then Mr Bell.' He eased the officer into what had been his seat before taking the chair beside Doctor Masters who raised a protest.

'There are obvious exceptions Julius!'

Lord Stirling shook his head. 'No, all names go on the list and as soon as we can prove that they had no motive, means or opportunity then they will be taken off the list. Is that how it works Mr Bell?'

'Yes my Lord, exactly like that.' Bell drew blank pages towards him, ready to find a killer.

'We need to know first when the jugs of cordial could have been tampered with. How far back do we have to go? Perhaps consider the people who were in Lord Caleb's room last night or were the jugs only placed in the room after everyone had gone down to the village for the wedding?' The officer glance briefly at the Earl but really was directing his question to the Butler.

'Fresh jugs were placed into Lord Delacourt's room at the same time as they were having breakfast. About 8 o'clock,' answered Preston.

'Good! That clears the evening activity in his Lordship's room with Noah and Adam Doyle. Now who prepares these jugs?' Bell dipped a quill into an ink well and made a note of the time.

'I do,' again answered Preston.

Bell glanced up, a little puzzled. 'I wouldn't have thought that was a normal duty for a Butler.'

A hint of a smile appeared as Preston inclined his head in agreement. 'One of my duties is to ensure the supply, stocking and dispensing of the wine cellar. With the Stirling household on an almost complete alcohol ban, I undertook it upon myself to supply tasty non-alcoholic alternatives. Mary also gave to the Doctor for testing samples of the concentrate cordials as well as the boiled water I use to mix up the jugs.'

Doctor Masters confirmed this. 'The concentrate and the plain water showed no indication of tampering.'

Bell was steadily writing down facts as they were revealed. 'So the tampering therefore must have taken place in Lord Caleb's room. Now then let's consider the victims as possible suspects.'

No Exceptions

A protest rose to Doctor Master's lips. 'Now really that is too much!'

Earl Stirling shook his head. 'No exceptions, Stanley. Bell doesn't know that this couldn't be a Romeo and Juliet situation until he can rule it out with evidence.'

'Thank you, my Lord. We can rule out the Shakespeare motive as neither family was against them marrying. Nor were either of them being pressured into this marriage. Also as they have been together almost the whole time they've been back at the Manor there was little opportunity for any of them to obtain the poison. So do we all agree that we have considered and can now reject Lord Caleb, Lady Tony and Lord Aidan as suspects?' He received four, 'Agreed.'

'Mary could have supplied the poison for her Ladyship.' *Having just agreed that Tony didn't have a motive to kill herself, her new husband and her baby brother, I feel like a traitor raising this point,* mused the Doctor.

'Let's consider Mary,' Bell suggested as he wrote her name on the list. 'Firstly I understand all about the scandal etc. surrounding the two abductions but neither of them were really being forced into this marriage were they?' Again he received four 'Agreed'. 'Then if Mary or anyone else poisoned them it was not upon their orders. For Mary, herself, she is a big loser with their deaths. She'll now have to find a new position, which would more than likely take her away from her lover William. He too loses the opportunity for advancement by joining Lord Caleb's staff. Oh, can we honestly say we are done with the Adam Doyle connection or is anyone else at the Manor related to him?'

Preston immediately answered, which surprised the Earl as he thought the Butler may have to think about the extensive staff on the estate. 'No one else has the last name Doyle or Sutherland here at the Manor or in the village.' At the Earl's look of surprise, Preston added, 'After last night's business with Adam and Noah I spent an hour going over employee records with Mrs Preston to be certain there were no more nasty surprises amongst the staff.'

'Good,' said Bell. 'That's another motive we can cross off the list. Now who else was in Lord Caleb's room this morning? Lady Isabella.' He looked up expecting the Doctor to protest but Masters was gripping his lips tightly together.

'Isabella was the one who told Caleb to talk to me about renewing his acquaintance with my daughter when he was going to see the colt I had for sale,' the Earl quietly stated. 'She may have had second thoughts after the scandals erupted but I certainly don't think Isabella would murder her own son especially after they have already married.'

'I totally agree, my Lord. Doctor Masters, I believe you re-bandaged Lord Caleb's eyes before they headed to the church.'

'Yes and although I may have been able to slip something into the room, I doubt someone would not have seen me put it into the jugs. I gain nothing from their deaths except sorrow that three beautiful young people have been taken from us before their time.'

Preston sighed, 'I too gain nothing.'

'Actually that's not true,' stated the Earl, 'You and Mary are named in Tony's will as is the Doctor. Just none of you are aware of that fact.'

'Are you sure about that, my Lord?' asked Bell. 'It does then give Mary a motive.'

The Earl sighed. 'No one knew as I made both Tony and Caleb make a will only last night. You see with Lizzy being rescued from her mother's and brother's tyranny, I'd been considering on settling some property or money onto Lizzy. To do this I needed to consider what amount of the un-entailed estate I would be giving Tony as her dowry as well as what I'd like to settle on Charlotte upon my death.' As Bell opened his mouth, the Earl added, 'Neither Charlotte or Lizzy know anything about that just yet.'

Who Benefits?

'Thank you, my Lord. What happens now to Lady Tony's dowry? Does it transfer to her husband upon their marriage, upon her death or revert back to the Stirling estate? Does it consist of a lot of money or property?'

'What I and her grandfather, Frederick Sinclair, bestow upon Tony remains her property and not her husband's. After bequests to various servants and villagers, the majority of Tony's estate will go to Heather Gray.'

'There was a moment of stunner silence. 'The Vicar's wife?' Bell queried as he wrote down the name.

'Yes, Heather is very passionate about the philanthropic work she does with giving girls and women a chance for a better life through education, training and a fresh start. To date Heather is limited by the need to seek donations and sponsors to open new schools, get housing for women in need. Tony wants Heather to not have to beg and scrounge for every penny she needs.'

'Were you happy with your daughter's decision, my Lord?'

'Absolutely! Every year I write Heather a big cheque and we open up the grounds here for a gala every Spring to raise money.'

'Are we talking about a lot of money from you and Mr Sinclair for her Ladyship's dowry? Would Mr Sinclair be in any financial constraints and wish to renege on giving away his money?'

A bark of a laugh came from Doctor Masters as the Earl smiled slightly. 'You obviously don't know who the Earl's father-in-law is,' laughed the Doctor. 'He's one of the wealthiest men in England without a title!'

Bell's eyebrows rose. 'Even wealthy men can lose money or fall on hard times.'

'Not this one!' said Masters, 'Sinclair's nickname in London is Midas because everything he touches turns to gold.'

'So, no, Frederick Sinclair is not interested in getting his money back,' concluded the Earl and Bell placed a cross next to Frederick's name on his list.

'Well, what about Lord Caleb's cousin, Geoff? I believe that he'll inherit the title is that correct?' Bell pressed on with his investigation.

'Yes,' said the Earl, 'He's the first real suspect. When Caleb and Geoff arrived to stay at the Manor, Geoff was shown all over the house as they were here to protect my children. He may have seen a cleaning product or poison that he could use.'

'Hum,' Bell was writing furiously, 'we have motive and means but do we have opportunity? Surely someone would have seen him tamper with the jugs? Did Mr Delacourt come downstairs with the rest of Lord Caleb's' group?'

Preston's eyes opened wide in surprise. 'No, he said he had to get something from his room and came down just before Lady Tony's party joined the gentlemen.'

'So is he the guilty person then?' asked the Doctor. 'What about this sighting of Agnes Henry?'

Shaking his head, Bell smiled. 'Not so fast Doctor Masters, we have a few more people to consider before we jump to any conclusions. Now did any of the ladies in Lady Antonia's room while she dressed, go into Lord Caleb's room this morning? Aside from his mother?'

Preston thought about it for a moment before he shook his head. 'No.'

'Did all the ladies come down together?'

'Yes.'

'What about Lady Charlotte and her sister Miss Henry?' asked Bell, making more notes as he spoke.

'They were in Charlotte's room when I went to collect them but Lizzy went back to her room for smelling salts for Charlotte and met us downstairs,' said the Earl.

'Are you positive that neither Lady Charlotte nor Miss Henry could have known about the money you were arranging for them?'

99

'Now really!' The Doctor's rant was interrupted by the Earl laying his hand upon his shoulder.

'It's' all right Stanley. They weren't present as I discussed it with Tony and Caleb and my lawyer, Clive Dunn, who came down from London this morning. But that isn't to say someone may have been listening at a keyhole.'

Glancing up with his pen poised Bell chose his next words carefully. 'I'm afraid it does mean that Miss Henry has a motive, opportunity and probably means, my Lord.'

Taking a deep breath, the Earl nodded. 'Solid suspect number two. Let's continue Bell.'

'Now I believe that the Moreau brothers and Madame Martin arrived this morning,' Bell glanced up at Preston who nodded.

'I offered them the opportunity to freshen up as their bags were carried upstairs but as they were worried about being late for the ceremony, they never went further than the entrance hall.'

'Good,' said Bell, 'so they had no opportunity and although the French visitors who crossed the Channel with you may have had the means and opportunity, I see no motive.'

Doctor Masters thoughtfully stroked his chin. 'Waterloo.' He said quietly.

Almost immediately the Bow Street Runner shook his head. 'There were plenty of chances in Paris to get their revenge if that was the case.'

'Begging your pardon sir,' Preston cleared his throat, 'but I see a flaw in your argument. In Paris did the Moreau brothers realise the masqueraders' true identity? Also Lord Caleb was on high alert for danger but once home, it would be expected he would drop his guard.'

'Fair point,' agreed the Earl, steepling his fingers together. 'But by the time the Moreaus came to our rescue in Dieppe, they knew the truth. If it was revenge they wanted they had us outmanned and out-gunned. Nor do I think they would have permitted their only sister to travel back to England with us.'

'Does your cousin Phillippe Du Bois benefit from Lady Tony's, Lord Aidan's or your death, my Lord?' Bell asked.

'Nothing of significance.'

'He wasn't jealous that Lady Tony was marrying another man?' Bell continued to write.

'No Phillippe has always been like a favourite uncle.'

'Well, that leads us to the Honourable Mr Patrick Stirling,' said Bell, pausing to flex his writing hand for a moment.

'Mr Patrick arrived from London before the Moreau party,' stated Preston, 'went up to his room to change and left the Manor before the French visitors arrived.'

Bell's eyebrows rose as he glanced up at the Butler, 'You say that as if it is significant.'

Preston nodded. 'Yes Sir, when Lord Caleb and Lady Tony returned from the church, they told me everything that had taken place there. Including the fact that Lord Caleb had been talking with the Moreau party for at least five to ten minutes before he noticed Mr Patrick arriving.'

Deep in thought Bell stroked his chin. 'Mr Stirling had opportunity to put the poison into the jugs when he went up to change but what was he doing between the time he left here and arrived at the church?'

The Doctor was becoming a little impatient and stated bluntly, 'What about Agnes Henry?'

Smiling, Bell wasn't put out by Masters' directness. 'We know from Mr Preston that one of the servants had seen a woman running away from the Manor and Mr Patterson and his brother offered to track her down. You found Mrs Henry then Mr Patterson?'

Solitaire's Report

Solitaire had been standing silently, in front of the French windows, staring out at the lovely array of Summer blooms that would cheer any heart. Except perhaps not one listening to how three young lives had been tragically taken away. He turned now and cleared his throat.

'Gerry and I were on horseback so we should've been only minutes behind the mystery woman. We half expected to be led to where a coach may have laid in wait but we ended up at a barn just on the outskirts of the estate and not far from the village.' There was a pause as the ex-Highwayman carefully chose his next words.

'Inside the barn was a gig and a horse, but also the dead body of Mrs Agnes Henry. It looks like she must have caught her foot on a half hidden piece of farm equipment and fallen, her head being cleavered open on the upturned blade.'

Bell was busy writing but Doctor Masters was particularly interested in Solitaire's choice of words.

'"Looks like she must have caught her foot and fallen?" Was there something that made you doubt this had in fact occurred?'

Solitaire stroked a hand across his chin. 'We would've been only moments if not seconds behind a woman on foot but we heard no scream, no cry out and the lady was dead; not dying. You'd know better than us, Doc, but there seemed to be too much blood spreading across the floor of the barn if it had only just occurred.'

'My word!' exclaimed the Doctor. 'Perhaps Agnes was already dead when a person dressed up like her was seen running away from the Manor. It could account for the time difference between Patrick leaving here and arriving at the church.'

Have We Forgotten Anyone?

The Earl had shown no sign of distress at either the news that his mother-in-law was dead or how she had died. 'Unfortunately it doesn't necessarily rule out Lizzy or Geoff. Lizzy disappeared for a good ten to twenty minutes and Geoff was seen outside the church smoking a cigar but there's no one to verify if he stayed there or could have sprinted back up to the house.'

'Well the first thing I need to do is inspect this barn with the Doctor who may be able to give me a more precise time of death. Mr Patterson, I'll need you to show us the way,' said Bell.

Solitaire nodded as Bell completed his writing, 'I left Gerry there to guard the scene.'

As Bell began to rise out of his chair, Doctor Masters interrupted. 'Haven't you forgotten someone? Duncan Gray?'

Bell looked a little bewildered. 'Lord Aidan's Tutor and the Reverend Gray's son?'

The Earl added quietly, 'Matthew is one of my oldest and dearest friends. He is a paragon in the community as is his wife Heather.'

Glancing sideways at the Earl, Doctor Masters chose his words carefully. 'You can't contribute the father's virtues onto the son, Julius. He may have had the means and opportunity to poison those children but…'

Bell finished for the Doctor, 'I don't see at this moment a motive for the murder.'

'He was in love with Lady Tony,' suggested the Doctor.

'But Duncan knew that the world he was about to enter into was not one suitable for Tony,' admitted the Earl. 'He told me so himself.'

Preston added, 'For several months now Mr Duncan has been receiving parcels, letters and various documents from London to work upon. Now that Mrs Gray has recovered, the

Government are very keen to have Mr Duncan work full time in one of their Foreign Office departments.'

The Earl agreed. 'In fact during the last war with Napoleon, Duncan had to spend sometimes a whole week at a time this past year up in London. Treaties with various nations to work together to beat Napoleon once and for all. The problem was the best of our fighting men were being held up with the conflict with the colonies in America which meant Wellington was left with less than desirable troops. There was the co-ordination of various spies and contacts in France. Duncan has the most amazing intellect,' Stirling said with more than just a little pride.

Doctor Masters blinked twice as he stared suddenly at his friend. 'And yet Julius, you were able to beat him at chess.'

A laugh escaped from the Earl. 'I sometimes think he did that to humour me.'

Bell looked at the Earl, deep in thought, before he added Duncan Gray's name to the bottom of his list and finally stood up. 'My Lord, you should be aware that you and Lady Charlotte could also be in danger. If you were to die now would Mr Patrick automatically become Earl?'

'No, a trust would take over until Charlotte gives birth. If the child is a son, he would inherit, if a daughter then Patrick would become Earl,' explained Lord Stirling.

Slowly Bell nodded. 'Unless you're both killed as well as the unborn child. Be careful what you eat and drink my Lord. Also it might be time to tell Lady Charlotte about the four deaths.'

'I'd rather wait until she is stronger, I'll have to also inform her about her mother's death.'

The Doctor said pragmatically as he arose out of his seat. 'Well you'll have to say something when you give the orders that Lady Charlotte's meals will have to be tasted before she is allowed to eat.'

A groan came from the Earl. 'As if Charlotte didn't already have enough problems about eating as it is.' Pulling himself together, he also stood up. 'I advise you Mr Bell to talk with my lawyer who is still here, as he has all the up to date wills as well as the changes I was planning on making to my own will and the estate.'

Bell bowed his head. 'Very good, my Lord. I'll catch up with Mr Dunn once I've been to the barn.'

With a heavy heart, Earl Stirling followed the four men out of his library. Preston showed Bell, Doctor Masters and Solitaire out the front door as reluctantly the Earl started to ascend the stairs up to his wife's bedroom.

Geoff's Despair

Linking his arm through Rosemary's, Andre Guillaume strolled along the patio towards the aromatic and colourful rose garden. After an hour of sitting with Mary in Caleb's bedroom, Andre felt Rosemary could do with some fresh air. They had just passed a large and ancient elm tree where they discovered Geoff Delacourt leaning against the huge trunk, smoking a cigar. He was in such a deep study that he jumped when Andre spoke.

'How are you holding up Lord Delacourt?'

Geoff turned startled, then angry eyes towards the French couple. 'Don't call me that!'

Glancing amazed from Geoff's suddenly flushed countenance to Rosemary and then back again, Andre apologised, 'I'm sorry if I have upset you but if Caleb is dead...'

Geoff didn't allow him to finish. 'I know! I know! I... I won't believe it until I have seen their bodies for myself!'

'It's not advisable, my Lord,' Rosemary added softly.

'Certainly Aunt Bella mustn't see them but... it's not like they had their faces blown off is it? I mean they're just not breathing right?'

Tears in her eyes, Rosemary shook her head at how normal Geoff wanted them to appear. 'No Sir, it's not how you want to remember them.'

Drawing hard on his cigar, Geoff's other hand ran distractedly through his hair, ruffling it so it looked like he'd just risen from his bed. 'So what the hell do we do now? That Bow Street Runner is still here isn't he? Patrick thinks the Countess' mother Agnes Henry was actually seen on the estate.'

Andre spread his hands in a very Gaelic gesture as he shrugged his shoulder. 'I am not in the Officer's confidences, my Lord. Madame Henry certainly had reason to be angry over the death of her son but to murder three people?'

Shaking his head, Geoff blew out another puff of smoke. 'Haven't you heard? The note telling Adam Doyle how to get Sutherland out of custody and kidnap Tony a second time was actually signed by Agnes Henry.'

'Oui,' there was a great deal of hesitation in that one word being drawn out by Andre, 'but that plan was to get control over Aidan and his inheritance. Now Agnes will have to wait until Lady Charlotte gives birth to ensure that they have any claim to the Stirling fortune.'

'Oh!' Rosemary looked up at Andre in surprise, 'So Monsieur Patrick isn't automatically Lord Stirling's heir?'

'No, but that is easily fixed!' The curtness of Geoff's tone caused both Andre and Rosemary to look at him surprised. Geoff coughed and his lips twisted into a wry smile. 'Sorry. It's just... after everything they've been through the past fortnight they had finally managed to get married and ... they didn't get to enjoy even one night as husband and wife!'

'And young Aidan... still just a babe and his life has been stolen from him. I... I don't know if I'd rather have a pistol handy when Bell discovers who did this, or strangle them with my bare hands!' His voice broke as he choked up with the emotion he had been valiantly trying to suppress.

Surprising both men, Rosemary wrapped her arms around Geoff and hugged him tightly, caressing her hand against his hair. Geoff stood stock still in shock for a moment but it wasn't long before his arms encircled Rosemary and he buried his face into her shoulder.

'What you need is some physical activity,' Andre suggested, 'I believe there's an exercise room here and a punching bag. Spend some time hitting an inanimate object and it might ease your desire to actually kill someone.' Sympathetically Andre patted Geoff on the back.

'I might just do that.' Geoff wiped a shaky hand over his eyes as he released Rosemary. 'I think I'll check on my aunt before I tackle some stress release.' Geoff stubbed out his cigar and nodding to the couple, he headed back into the Manor. Taking Rosemary's hand, Andre continued their interrupted stroll.

'Well? What do you think?' Rosemary looked up at Andre to find him wearing a frown.

'I don't know ma cherie. I'm glad it is Monsieur Bell and not I who must uncover the true culprit. Shall we pick some roses to brighten and freshen up Caleb's room? It might put a smile on Mary's face for all of a second.'

When Rosemary giggled and nodded, Andre gestured to a nearby gardener who found a basket and a pair of secateurs for them.

Patrick's Anguish

The stables were a hive of activity as all the horses were being led out into a paddock for some exercise. Phillippe had just been to see the new foal and was about to follow the Groom who was leading the mother, Caviar, and her newborn out to a separate paddock from the other horses when Patrick came up from the house.

'Who's available for a ride Simon?' Patrick stopped the Groom who was leading the mare and her foal.

'I'm sorry Mr Patrick but Officer Bell's orders are that no one is to leave the estate.'

A frown descended upon Patrick's brow as he twitched his rider's crop between his fingers. 'I only want some exercise. I'm not fleeing the crime scene! What he doesn't know can't hurt him huh?' An attractive smile replaced his frown but the Groom was adamant in his refusal.

'Sorry Mr Patrick but Lord Stirling asked that we do everything we can to assist Mr Bell's investigation.'

Patrick's lips thinned and a muscle twitched along his jaw and Phillippe took pity on the younger man as he linked his arm through his cousin's.

'Come on Patrick, let's go and watch Caviar and her new foal, Blue Moon, as they run around their paddock.' Nodding to Simon to continue, the two men fell in behind the mare and foal.

For a while Patrick walked beside Phillippe in silence, a frown marring his usual quizzical expression until what Phillippe had just said finally sunk in.

'Blue Moon? What an unusual choice of name. As in "Once in a blue moon"? Tony usually chose words associated with black for the pure black horses.' Patrick's voice had quavered slightly as he had said his deceased cousin's name but Phillippe pretended that he hadn't noticed.

'The night Blue Moon was born was a full moon. As a moon's cycle is every 28 days and we have 30 to 31 days in most months, there are months when one of the four phases can occur more than once. Therefore on rare occasions there can be two full moons in the one month. The second full moon is called a Blue Moon. That was when this foal was born.' Phillippe leant against the fence as Simon released Caviar's reins and closed the gate behind him as he left mother and son to enjoy the green grass, sunshine and fresh air.

For a while the new foal wouldn't leave his mother's side but as his confidence grew and his curiosity overcame his fear, Blue Moon started to explore his new surroundings.

Phillippe found the peace and calm of the scene interrupted by the nervous agitated energy that was radiating from Patrick. He really needed something physical to distract him from the horror that he kept living. *It hadn't been easy watching Tony marry another man but I had reconciled myself to the fact that my cousin really loved someone else. That another man would be kissing her, touching her, making love... but now they were no longer breathing. Tony would be gone completely from my life. Her body now nothing but an empty beautiful shell that would quickly begin to rot away from her bones.*

Shaking his head Patrick tried to think of something else, anything other than this image of decay and loss. When Phillippe placed a sympathetic hand on Patrick's shoulder, he jumped startled as he had forgotten his French cousin's presence beside him.

'Sorry Phillippe, I'm not very good company at the moment. You must feel doubly empty, first your father and now Tony and Aidan. I was wondering if I should go and offer my support to Grandmama but I don't know if I'd be of any comfort to her.'

Phillippe shook his head. 'My mother is with Aunt Margarette and I believe Patience Sinclair is comforting Isabella. I was being annoying just sitting there. Women grieve differently and apparently I was cramping their grieving process. So like you I thought I'd go for a ride but...' Phillippe spread his hands expressively as he shrugged.

Glancing away from his French cousin, Patrick was unable to stop the rise of the feeling of envy that he often felt at how easily the fluid grace of Gaelic charm and mannerisms came to Phillippe. Something he had worked so hard to cultivate.

'Well, there's still the option of bribing Preston to let us have access to the wine cellar and drink till we pass out.' Although Patrick said it in a jovial tone, the idea had already seriously crossed his mind more than once since he had heard the horrific news.

Turning away from the scene of a young colt exploring his paddock, Phillippe placed both his hands upon Patrick's shoulders. 'Mon cousin, considering the family history of alcoholism do you really want to start down that road? Have we not lost enough members of our family this day?'

Looking away from the seriousness in Phillippe's eyes, Patrick felt suddenly so very much younger than his cousin. He tried to laugh but even to his ears it sounded forced.

'I didn't really mean it.'

Phillippe refused to release Patrick as he shook his head. 'Oh but you did, mon cousin! You would like to wipe this day completely from your memory. It is possible that you could learn to live with Tony marrying someone else but to lose her completely from your life… forever… that makes you feel like your heart has been torn out of your chest. You want something, anything to stop you thinking, to stop you feeling but no matter what you choose, it can't obliterate that memory forever… except death.'

Dragging in a sharp breath, Patrick looked up into his cousin's concerned face and wondered if the Frenchman was some sort of wizard. *Unable to take the hushed ambiance of the Manor I had the wild and crazy thought as I strode out to the stables, of riding really hard and fast, of my horse tossing me or faulting at a jump and me falling and breaking my neck! If I can't bear the grief for the loss of my beautiful cousin, then I could join her in eternal rest.*

'I… I don't know what you mean.' Patrick found it difficult to maintain eye contact with Phillippe. His cousin didn't force the issue, he had seen the look of acknowledgement on Patrick's face when he mentioned death and released Patrick's shoulders.

'At stressful times like this I find the reinforcement of new life to be soothing.' Phillippe gestured to the new born colt. 'If

I'm suffering from nervous energy then I find the art of fencing very therapeutic.'

Patrick burst out laughing. 'I never could understand your fixation for duelling. You and Tony could practice for hours and I never understood how she could look so... exhilarated after a session with you.'

An enigmatic smile appeared on Phillippe's face as he stroked his chin. 'Oui, I'm certain that you would've seen a similar look on our cousin's features if she had been allowed to consummate her marriage with Caleb.'

Patrick stumbled backwards slightly as he gasped in surprise. 'Are you saying that you and Tony got up to more than just fencing or that fencing can be as good as an orgasm?'

'The latter, please Patrick, I'm old enough to be Tony's father! My eldest son Christoph is nearly 17, Dominic is 15 and Georgette is 13.'

Phillippe's Story

Leaning back against the fence, Patrick was happy to be distracted from his thoughts about suicide. 'I forgot you were married. You didn't consider an arranged marriage between Christoph and Tony once your son was a little older of course?'

Taking his enamel cigar case out of his pocket, Phillippe paused in raising a cigar to his lips as he swept a searching glance over his cousin.

'I will not be arranging marriages for any of my children! In fact when Julius wrote to me explaining his plan to throw Tony and Caleb together I warned him of the dangers of loveless arranged marriages.' Lighting his cigar, Phillippe had surprised Patrick by the bitterness of his tone.

'They have been known to work for many couples.' *I wonder why I feel I am standing on thin ice?*

'In my case, it did not! Florence felt that she had done her duty to our marriage and to motherhood by producing as she put it, "an heir, a spare and a daughter." So she left us to pursue her dreams as playing happy family was stifling her creativity.'

'I'm so sorry. I don't remember any of this.'

Phillippe shrugged. 'We kept it very quiet especially after what eventually happened.'

Squinting as he thought hard, Patrick unconsciously ran his hand through his hair, messing up his carefully perfect hair style.

'Hold on, Andre Guillaume mentioned that his wife's name was Florence and that she was a Du Bois. I thought he meant it was her maiden name. He didn't mean your wife did he? I thought you Frenchmen were Catholic and couldn't divorce?'

Phillippe smoked for a moment before he finally answered, 'It was easier for the children if they didn't know their mother had abandoned them so it was better if it wasn't widely known in society that my wife and the "wife" of Andre were in fact the same woman.'

'But I've seen you with Guillaume and it seems like you're friends.'

'We were and still are friends. Florence had a passion for the Arts. Painters, poets, sculptors and play writers were forever littering our house. Andre and I had been friends since childhood so naturally my door was always open to him. Because he could be locked away writing for months at a time, we saw him only at intervals.'

'Florence had barely taken any real notice of Andre until after Georgette was born and she decided that was too bourgeois for the bohemian lifestyle she wanted. Andre moved easily amongst that class and because he was friendly but kept Florence at arm's length, she set about seducing him.'

As his cousin disclaimed in disbelief, Phillippe puffed on his cigar. 'But he was your friend!'

Phillippe shrugged. 'Even better for Florence as she really wanted to hurt me, especially whenever I didn't go along with her impossible hare brained schemes. Andre did what he could to distance himself from Florence's obvious pursuit but as he had always admired her, she preyed upon that weakness. She told all manner of lies about me, from abusing her, starving her in the attic, to shooting her favourite mare. That last one was actually true.'

Horrified Patrick cast a quick glance behind him, wondering for the safety of Caviar and Blue Moon. Phillippe shook his head. 'No, I'm not crazy, Florence easily left out of her story that she had ridden her horse towards a wall intending to scale it but rammed the poor horse straight into it. The mare broke both her front legs, she had to be put down.'

'Oh that's different! You couldn't do anything else.' Patrick couldn't help it, he was visibly relieved.

The emotions were still, even now, so raw that a muscle twitched along Phillippe's jaw line as he smoked in silence until he had regained control of himself. 'When Florence's wild stories started circulating Paris, I knew that I had to finally do something. There was no way Andre would repeat her tall stories but it was obvious that he was not the only one she was telling them to. I didn't care what she said about me, but it was starting to affect my father's standing as a well-respected Senator.'

'Then Florence went too far, she said that the children were never seen with her as they were deformed or ugly monsters. When François' father died in prison and Julius was treading the dangerous waters with his Irish relatives, no one but Julius and I knew who or where François was located. Endangering not only the safety of Louise and François but also her own children, Florence sent word to the Irish cousins where they could find the ten year old heir to their title. That was it, I was done with her games and treachery. I sent the children with Louise, François and my mother over to Julius while I and father remained in Paris to deal with François' cousins. Blood was spilt but my father promised that even more would be spilt if they did not return home and resume their negotiations with Julius.'

'Florence had been banished to the country house but when she was permitted to return to Paris, she was no longer my wife! People assumed that she had been sent away with the children to England for safety – assumed or were prepared to look the other way that the same woman returned but with a different name. So Florence got her wish she could join the artisans but there was a cost to be paid.'

'She never saw her children again and many of the doors of the upper and middle classes were now shut to her. To some functions Andre was welcome but Florence was not. Andre paid the highest price, even though he was horrified at what she had done, he did truly love her and agreed to protect her from her wild disregard for anyone else.'

Totally enthralled by the story, Patrick had forgotten for the moment his own grief. 'That doesn't sound like Andre was very successful in keeping her under control. Both of you talk about her in the past tense.' Phillippe squared his shoulders and Patrick wondered how much worse this story could get.

'The bohemians were rather loose on the idea of marriage and monogamy. So as soon as one man or... even woman became attractive to Florence, she just had to have them. She always returned to the protection supplied by Andre and he managed to get her to remember to use... birth control but these artisans were also into heavy drinking, experimenting with drugs and ... orgies.'

'When I walked away from Florence I warned her that I'd accept no bastards bearing my family's name. That was one thing we both agreed on, although for different reasons. She hated being pregnant and losing the admiration that she thought was her due. So she tried very hard to remember to use the sponges or douching or whatever it is women use to prevent pregnancy but with the drinking, the drugs and the orgies it became easy to forget even what day it was.'

'Andre had been forced to leave Florence with her current lover and his "wife" when he had to go into the country as his mother was dying. He thought to be gone only two or three days but it was seven days before his mother died and then there were the funeral arrangements. Meanwhile Florence had participated in a drug hazed week long orgy. The upshot was that she now found herself pregnant, in denial and couldn't claim that the child was Andre's as she had stopped sharing his bed after the first couple of months, more than two years prior.;

'She hid the truth from Andre until she had started to show. I reluctantly said I would take the child but my name would not appear on the birth certificate and although it couldn't be Andre's, the child would bear his name. Being pregnant had always made Florence feel she was fat and ugly so she continued to try anything she could to lose the baby. It was like this child was consuming her from the inside and she just had to get it out.'

'So Florence didn't even ask any questions or tell Andre when one of the women took her to a "Doctor" who could take care of her little problem. She barely made it back through Andre's door before she started haemorrhaging. A real Doctor was sent for but the butcher had done too much damage as Florence had been further along in her pregnancy than most of the women he usually 'fixed''. The child was still born which was actually a relief as he was horribly deformed.'

'The Doctor explained that wasn't because he was premature but because Florence had contracted and left untreated syphilis. She had thought all the symptoms of the disease had been actually related to her pregnancy. Even at the end, Florence had lost too much blood for the Doctor to save her; she blamed everyone else for what had befallen her. Even poor Andre for being away while his mother was dying. He was shattered by Florence's death. It was nearly a whole year before he could pick up a quill again. That was nearly ten years ago and it is still difficult for Andre to discuss.'

Wiping his handkerchief across his face, Patrick was visibly moved by his cousin's story. 'Good grief Phillippe, you need to get Andre away from here as soon as possible! To be subjected to more pointless deaths must be torture for him!'

Phillippe stubbed out the butt of his cigar. 'Unfortunately we're all tied here until Monsieur Bell solves these murders!' He was pleased by the humanity he had seen expressed by his usually cynical, self-absorbed cousin and now put his arm around Patrick's shoulder. 'Come! I'm going to show you what you've been missing with fencing.' Leaving Blue Moon to continue to explore his big wide world, they headed back up to the house.

François' Insistence

Knocking upon the door of the school room, François stepped inside even before his knock had been acknowledged. 'Oh no, Monsieur Duncan, this is not right.' François strode forward towards the main desk in the room where Duncan Gray had been busily writing. A shade of annoyance sat upon the Tutor's face as he reluctantly raised his eyes to the beautiful young man.

'Too true but you're already in now!' drawled Duncan, laying his quill down as François laughed at his quip.

'Oh how you tease! That isn't what I meant and you know it. You shouldn't be cooped up here all alone. Surrounded by nothing but memories of your late pupil.'

One of Duncan's eyebrows rose at the Frenchman's concerned manner. 'I have plenty of work to keep me distracted. Is there something you want? Otherwise I'm quite busy.' His other eyebrow rose as François sat down on the opposite side of the desk.

'You English, always the stiff upper lip. It is important that you release all that emotion that is boiling up inside of you before...' He demonstrated with his hands an explosion.

A wry smile twisted Duncan's lips. 'Before I turn into a Frenchman?'

François gasped and then laughed. 'Oh you're so naughty.' That last word made François remember Tony and his smile slid away. 'Sorry that was the word Andre used to describe how amorous Tony and Caleb managed...' the French god looked away as he wiped a tear from his eyes. In sympathy Duncan laid his hand over the top of François' but his words were less supportive.

'If this is an example of the maudlin emotions you want me to indulge in then forgive me but I'll pass.'

François wasn't so easily deterred. 'Non, non, it's just the association of that one word with Tony made it all too real... this horrific act someone has committed. We all loved Tony, but it must be even harder for you as you were in love with her weren't you?'

Duncan's breath caught in a sharp inhalation. *It is a fine distinction François has just made and it has cut close to the quick.* 'Therefore what? That I must be hurting even more than anyone else in this house? Or are you suggesting that because I couldn't have her, I killed her, her husband and little brother for good measure?' There was more than a hard edge to Duncan's voice at the suggestion that he could destroy the woman he loved.

A look of hurt entered François' eyes. 'I would never suggest anything so base! I came to you knowing that you were in love with Tony, you couldn't talk to anyone openly about the pain of your loss without it perhaps being misinterpreted. I do know and understand and offer you someone you may talk to without fearing I would judge or demean the strong feelings that you carry.'

For a moment Duncan could only study François' face but was unable to detect any signs of mockery or deceit. Very slowly Duncan exhaled and his rigid posture relaxed slightly. 'That is very kind of you François but that wound is still… too raw. I feel… so helpless. What could we have done differently to prevent this nightmare? Who could have done this? Why now that they had finally found happiness?'

'I want to help Mr Bell but I feel I'm tearing my hair out, trying to think this through logically. I'm a scholar and not a man of action but right now I need desperately to be doing something, anything! My brains have failed me so I need to be physically involved in this hunt. I want to hurt someone for taking not just one beautiful soul away from us, but three! I need to feel pain as I'm inflicting it upon this monster!' Duncan had to pause to drag in a deep breath before he passed out as he let some of his pent up emotions loose.

In one fluid movement of grace, François rose out of his chair, moved around the desk and drew Duncan up into a hug. At first Duncan just stood there, dragging in deep breaths as he tried to regain his composure. When François continued to hug him, Duncan tried to push the Frenchman away but François' grip tightened.

'That's it mon ami, take your frustration out on me!'

Duncan went very still. 'No! You've been abused enough! I won't hit you too. Please let me go now.'

Releasing Duncan, François kept his hands upon Duncan's shoulders. 'Bon, you've released some steam and logic is no longer alien to you. Come! Let us tackle something physical and it may make that great brain of your run like a thoroughbred once again.'

Nodding Duncan gathered together the papers he had been working on but paused when he was about to slide the notes into a top drawer.

'You're not talking about sex are you?'

François' smile was more than a little mischievous. 'Unless that is your pleasure, but non, that is not what I meant.'

Satisfied, Duncan locked away his notes and willingly followed François out of the school room.

Charlotte's Reaction

Inhaling deeply, the Earl entered his wife's apartments through her dressing room. *I feel like a moral coward but have promised myself that if Charlotte is sleeping then I will come back later with my devastating news.* Easing his head around the doorway into the bedroom his wish to delay telling his wife of the deaths was dashed. Charlotte was sitting up in bed, wearing a dressing gown and enjoying a plate of fruits and assorted delicacies that had once graced the reception table downstairs. Charlotte smiled up at her husband and waved a small hand towards her sister who sat in one of the arm chairs beside the bed.

'I feel so much better now Julius. Doctor Masters gave me a little tonic and I was just about to send Lizzy down to join in the celebrations. I must admit I'm surprised at how little I can hear of the party downstairs which I thought would make my head ache and I wouldn't be able to sleep.'

Lizzy had obediently risen from her chair but the Earl laying his hand gently on his sister-in-law's shoulder eased her back into her chair.

'Stay Lizzy, please, I'll probably need your help,' said the Earl. 'The reason why you can't hear any party, Lotte, is because there isn't one.'

Blinking up at her husband Charlotte wiped her hands on a napkin. 'Why not? There hasn't been yet another abduction surely?'

Earl Stirling sat down on the edge of his wife's bed. 'No, not that. We believe that while we were at the church someone stole into the house and added poison to the jugs of cordials kept in Caleb's room. I'm... I'm afraid that Caleb, Tony and Aidan all partook of one of the cordials once they returned from the wedding... They're... they're all dead!'

As to be expected there was a stunned silence as the two women in the room tried to process what the Earl had just said. Lizzy gasped and pressed her hand against her mouth as her eyes filled with tears. Charlotte just stared blindly up at her husband.

'No! No that can't be! You must send for Doctor Masters, Julius, there... there may still be time to do something... anything, to save them!' Charlotte reached out hands like taloned claws to grasp the Earls jacket by the lapels.

Laying his hands over the top of her cold ones, Earl Stirling slowly shook his head. 'Doctor Masters was with me when they were discovered. There was nothing that he could do!' As tears welled in his beautiful wife's eyes, the Earl's resolve to remain strong was beginning to crumble.

'Who?' Lizzy demanded through her own tears, 'Who has done this vile deed?'

Shaking his head, the Earl glanced across at his sister-in-law. 'Bell is working on that now.'

Whisking her handkerchief out of the sleeve of her gown, Lizzy tried to wipe away her tears but they continued to fall. 'Thank goodness Mother must be still in London or she'd be a prime suspect.'

'Lizzy how could you? Poor Mama!' Charlotte lashed out at her sister, accepting the handkerchief that her husband placed into her trembling hand.

'Actually one of the servants saw someone running away from the house this morning that matched Agnes.' The Earl admitted. Both sisters gawked at him,

'No!' Lizzy said in disbelief. 'If she is responsible, Julius, then she must be stopped. There's no saying who she could try to eliminate next.'

Which brought the Earl to his next bit of bad news. 'Well that may not be necessary. The woman's trail led to a barn where your mother's body has allegedly been found. It looks like she tripped and fell, hitting her head on some farming implements. Doctor Masters has gone there now and will be able to make a more positive identification before we're certain that it is in fact your mother.'

When Charlotte let out a howl of disbelief the Earl jumped startled and Lizzy firmly grabbing his arm, pulled him out of the way as she placed a basin on the bed beside her sister. As the tears, the howling and the uncontrolled limbs of hysteria began, the Earl automatically removed the plate out of Charlotte's reach and stepped back just in time as her body began to reject her recent meal.

Backing strategically towards the door as Lizzy struggled to contain Charlotte's unruly arms as she held the bowl steady, the Earl felt like a miserable coward, this time for wishing to desert the repugnant scene. *I should make the effort to at least offer my assistance to Lizzy.* The Earl was saved by the arrival of Jane, Charlotte's Maid. Hearing her mistress begin to howl in grief, Jane had run down the corridor and now guided the Earl out of the door.

'There's nothing more you can do, my Lord.' Shutting him out of the room, Jane joined Lizzy in ministering to Charlotte's distress. As the Earl sought sanctuary somewhere much more quiet, he longed unrealistically for the return of his wife. *My first wife, Grace – Tony's mother. Grace had lost six children through miscarriage, three through still birth and four babies who had barely made it past two years of age; and yet although Grace had grieved the loss of each and every one of her babies, it had never made me flee in discomfort. I just hoped that Bell is able to solve this murder mystery before anyone else becomes a victim.*

The Sensual Art Of Fencing

As Phillippe and Patrick stepped into the gymnasium through a pair of French doors, Geoff had just taken off his jacket and waistcoat, throwing them over the back of a chair before he started to roll up his sleeves. He looked up surprised as the cousins entered the room and paused with one sleeve half rolled up.

'Sorry I didn't realise anyone else would be here,' said Geoff, 'I don't want to get in the way. It was suggested that I could work off my negative energy by punching the living daylights out of an inanimate object.'

Closely watching both Geoff and Patrick without really seeming to, Phillippe held out his hand to detain Geoff. 'Please don't leave on our account. I think we can all do with some stress release.'

Patrick readily agreed and all three men looked around as Duncan and François entered from inside the house.

'Well, well,' said Phillippe with a smile, 'it would seem two more gentlemen have the need to let off some steam.' He gestured for the new comers to enter but with stiff little bow, Duncan turned on his heels and strode out of the room.

'Wait mon ami,' called out François, 'let us go for a walk instead while the sun does shine.' In answer to the silent nod from Phillippe, François ran after Duncan and led him outside. The three remaining gentlemen looked at each other in surprise.

'If he was any more tightly wound,' Geoff drawled, 'I think he'd burst at the seams.'

Removing his jacket, Patrick nodded. 'I've always found Duncan a little stiff and scholarly. You don't suppose that great brain of his has finally suffered a melt down?' He very carefully arranged his jacket over the back of a chair before removing his waistcoat.

Taking the epee swords out of their cabinet Phillippe tested one blade with a couple of swishes before making certain that both blades had their safety buttons firmly attached.

'No mon cousin, he was in love with Tony, like you and it's not easy for you English to express your feelings with a lot of people around.' It was just a statement of fact and Phillippe didn't expect an answer from either Englishman standing in front of him which was just as well as he wasn't about to get one.

'I'm about to instruct my young cousin here the sensuality of fencing and you're more than welcome to join us, Delacourt. Unless you particularly want to go ahead with your previous desire to knock the stuffing out of the punching bag?' There was just a touch of mockery to Phillippe's voice but his smile took away any sting his words may have carried.

Both of Geoff's eyebrows rose. The sensuality of fencing? If I'd known that I might have paid more attention to my lessons as a youth. If Patrick doesn't mind me watching?'

Taking one of the swords Phillippe held out to him Patrick immediately replied, 'I'd prefer you were my opponent than my cousin. We should be more evenly matched that way.'

Handing the other epee to Geoff, Phillippe cast a quick searching glance at Patrick. 'Is that an aspersion about my age?'

'Not in the way you may think,' Patrick hastened to reassure. 'It's just that you've spent a life time studying it as an art form that I doubt that either of us is a match for you.'

Making a couple of passes in the air, Geoff sighed. 'Caleb took more interest in fencing than I did. It would've been interesting to have seen you matched against him,' he told Phillippe who was removing his own jacket and waist coat.

The Frenchman smiled wistfully. 'Having taught Tony, all I know I would love to have seen her and Caleb cross swords. It would also have made it easier to explain the sensuality analogy.'

Clapping his hands together, Phillippe became more business-like. 'Limber up gentlemen, you need to loosen and warm up your muscles.' As he began to stretch his own leg muscles, Patrick looked at him quizzically.

'Is that really necessary?'

Phillippe stretched his arms over his head. 'Going cold into a fight can lead to torn tendons, strained muscles and damage to your neck and shoulders.' The two younger men followed his example of stretches but felt more than a little sheepish.

'Throughout the ballrooms of France and England a new dance is gaining popularity much to the horror of mothers and the narrow minded,' instructed Phillippe as he continued to stretch various parts of his body. 'The waltz is the first dance where a man and woman are in such close proximity to each other throughout the whole dance. His hand on her waist, his other hand clasping hers and their bodies so close together that mothers fear that it may lead to inappropriate behaviour from their young inexperienced daughters and lust-seeking sons.'

'The man leads, the woman follows, and it is so akin to the act of sexual intercourse that some houses refuse to permit the dance in their establishment. There's a sensuality underlining this dance that is blatantly obvious but it can also be seen subtly in the art of fencing. Now then gentlemen, turn and face your partner and check that the safety button is still firmly attached to your blade.'

Securing for himself a third blade, Phillippe cast a shrewd, appraising glance over the two waiting young men. Patrick cocked a quizzical eyebrow at Geoff who grinned and tried to not snigger.

'Gentlemen! Bow to your opponent.' Phillippe snapped their attention back to him and watched them both very closely. Geoff's bow was almost as stiff as Duncan's had been, ensuring that he never lowered his eyes away from Patrick's face. Phillippe nodded his approval but glancing across at Patrick, the

Frenchman was taken aback. With an elaborate flourish of his hand, Patrick was nearly bent right over.

'Non, non mon cousin! A thousand times non!' Phillippe protested, causing Patrick to jerk upright in surprise. 'You're not in ballroom now. Never expose your neck to your enemy. Your eyes should never leave his. This is not just a battle of the strength but the mind as well.'

'I thought,' drawled Geoff, 'that this was just about letting off some steam?'

'Oui, of course, but we are still gentlemen and we will conduct ourselves appropriately. This is a dance of a different kind. Assessing your opponent's weaknesses and strengths. Just as two potential lovers assess each other when they first meet.'

For a moment Patrick looked horrified. 'For their strengths and weaknesses? Surely not?'

'La, la! Don't be so literal mon cousin. In fencing the assessment is more blatant, in courtship, more subtle. If you're dancing with a woman and you discover that she will step on your foot every time at a certain point in the dance then you learn not to have your foot in that spot to be stepped upon. You learn, you adapt.'

'If the lady is worth the trouble you offer to practice with her until you're in sync with each other. It is the same with sexual intercourse. It is much nicer to have a partner who engages with you, rises to meet you rather than just lies there and expects you to do all the work.' Phillippe flexed his sword arm. 'So it is when fencing. You learn all that you can from your opponent, you adapt to utilise their weakness against them, and you want someone who will engage with you whole heartedly even if it is only practice.'

Withdrawing a handkerchief from his trouser pocket, Patrick mopped his brow at such an intimate discussion. 'You had this... orgasmic rush whenever you fence with Tony? How did you manage to not take your encounters from the bout to the bedroom?'

Phillippe threw him a look of scorn. 'The fact that I'm old enough to be her father? As much as I loved Tony, I never wanted to make love to her. Now if Caleb and Tony had ever fenced… Oui that could've been another form of foreplay for them.' Such a wistful look on the Frenchman's face caused Geoff to gasp.

'There was definitely nothing lover-like when we saw Tony cross swords with Nigel Sutherland when he ambushed them on their way home from Stirling Arms.'

Chuckling, Phillippe could easily imagine the scene as Caleb had described the encounter when he had first caught up with them at the Grand Duchess Hotel in Paris. 'Oui but Tony fought not in practice but to defend her life, her honour and her secret. Did you not think as you watched her that she didn't need your rescue?'

'Until she fell, yes,' agreed Geoff.

'When Nigel drew out his penis to humiliate Tony, was he not already erect? He had found the encounter stimulating and his win even more so.'

'Even though he didn't know that Tony was a Lady and not a Lord?' asked Patrick, appalled and yet intrigued.

'Oui, he had found not a weak opponent but one that challenged him. His win was cheap as it was an accident and not his skill that had overcome Tony's defence. Being the animal he is, Nigel took the win none the less and to prove to himself more so than to Tony. That he was the better man, he intended to humiliate her by… well we don't know his intent, to urinate on her but considering his arousal, probably ejaculate over her. Luckily for your timely arrival Nigel was unable to do either. Although the appearance of Solitaire could have also been in time to save Tony for humiliation.'

Pausing, Phillippe circled the two young Englishmen as he studied their physical similarities and differences.

'Surely there's nothing sexual about crossing swords with the enemy in battle?' asked Patrick, shocked at the idea of being aroused about killing another human being. Phillippe eyebrows rose as his thoughts had been assessing them as opponents.

'While it is your body that's involved in something so physical, your brain is not dormant. Chemicals are released during orgasm, different ones released when you're fighting for your life. Your instinct is to fight or flight. This is an impulse in the brain. Winning – whether it is a friendly bout, a serious fight to the death or finally convincing a beautiful young lady to your bed; they all trigger pleasure in your brain. Later there may be regret or remorse but at the time you're the victor.'

Running a careful finger along the blade in his hand, Geoff said in a thoughtful voice, 'So is the epee a metaphor for a penis? Or is your analogy more about the actual pursuit of your intended lover rather than the physical act of intercourse?'

Resting the tip of his blade lightly on the ground like a cane, Phillippe chuckled. 'The analogy may be relevant for either the pursuit or the act but until this moment I'd never thought of the sword as a substitute for my penis.'

Patrick stiffened suddenly as he recalled a conversation with his cousin as Tony had announced her engagement. 'When Tony was forced into dresses, she said she missed carrying a sword,' admitted Patrick. 'I teased her that it was less about protection and more the male appendage she lacked. It wasn't the reason of course but I just never understood how protective Tony was over Aidan.'

Biting into his bottom lip, Phillippe fought back the urge to make a very obvious comment. Geoff, though, wasn't so tactful.

'Really? With you being so blatantly obvious about wanting to become the next Earl?'

Phillippe's sharp intake of breath was an audible hiss as he said the typical fencing exclamation, 'Sa! Sa! Have at you!' Patrick immediately raised his blade as his cheeks blazed and Phillippe placed his own blade between the two men.

'La! La! Are you Delacourt then the rare being who has never envied another man his title, his woman or his money?' Phillippe forced the two men to take a step backwards from each other.

Geoff rubbed an agitated hand over the back of his neck. 'Envied, yes, coveted, no! I didn't want Caleb's title, his money or his beautiful wife, I... I just wanted...' He found it impossible to complete the sentence.

Phillippe's eyes narrowed as he scrutinised the turmoil on the young man's face. 'You wanted what you could never have; you wanted Caleb,' he said quietly. It was a simple statement rather than an accusation. Even so Geoff launched himself at Phillippe but his blade was easily parried away by the expert swordsman.

'Are you angry at me Delacourt or at yourself because you think it shameful to love another man?'

'It's un-natural.' Geoff admitted through gritted teeth. Patrick hadn't backed away from him in horror but he was looking at Geoff a little perplexed.

'La! La! One day, maybe not in our lifetime, there will be no shame attached to such a love. Do you think that when I saw that François was equally attracted to men as he was to women that I made him suppress his desires? Non, I encouraged him to develop this attraction. Being heir to a title, François will have to marry and beget a son, but that does not mean he should hide his natural instincts. Monogamy is not for everyone. Believe me, I know! But so long as your affairs are discreet there is no reason why you can't have both.'

Geoff sadly shook his head. 'That might only work if the person you're in love with is also that way inclined.'

Spreading his hands as he shrugged his shoulders in a very Gaelic manner, Phillippe sighed. 'I'm sorry, mon ami, but that I can't help you with.' Resuming his cooler, impartial tone, he added, 'Now are you boys still interested in fencing or have I totally drained your energy? It's such a warm day outside and there's a secluded watering hole that's just perfect for a dip.'

The two Englishmen looked at each other as if seeing the man opposite for the first time. Geoff thought, *We have learnt so much from Phillippe and about each other that we are no longer certain that we understand who our opponent really is. In the presence of this master, what else could we accidently let slip and reveal about ourselves? Instead of becoming more heated in battle, a chance to cool down and reinforce our protective shields might be a very good idea.* Dragging in a deep calming breath, Geoff stepped backwards.

'Actually, that's not a bad suggestion.'

Patrick was already passing his foil across to Phillippe. 'I agree but…'

Smirking, Geoff raised his hands innocently. 'You're perfectly safe from me. As I have one fixation, I know your fixation was your own cousin.'

Patrick opened his mouth to hotly refute the claim until he finally thought it all the way through. 'Oh you mean Tony, not Phillippe. That would be too weird!'

In the process of carrying all three swords back to their cupboard, Phillippe drawled, 'I'm right here you know! I may be older but I'm not deaf. Nor do I consider myself hideously ugly!'

'Sorry coz, but if I was going to turn for one of my own team then it would be someone like François. After all you are old enough to be my father.'

Locking up the cupboard, Phillippe sighed. 'You're not too old to be put over my knee and spanked.'

Removing his jacket from the back of a chair Patrick said in mock horror. 'No Daddy I'll be good!' Shrugging himself into his jacket Patrick added, 'I was going to suggest you spank Geoff but he'd probably enjoy it too much.'

Geoff paused in the process of rolling down his shirt sleeves. 'Don't drag me into your twisted fantasy! I'm not the one with daddy issues!'

Picking up his own jacket, Phillippe shoved the two younger men towards the French door. 'If you boys are intent upon bickering all afternoon I might just be tempted to drown you both.'

Glancing mischievously at each other, Patrick and Geoff grinned. 'You'll have to catch us first!' said Geoff before he and Patrick ran out into the garden like a pair of school boys. Shaking his head, Phillippe followed them to the watering hole at a more leisurely pace.

François' Secret Other Life

'Mon ami, wait up! What's the hurry?' François had to jog to catch up with Duncan as they headed out into the garden. 'To where are you running? Or should that be from what or whom are you running?'

Duncan stopped so suddenly that François cannoned into the back of him and had to place his hands on the Tutor's shoulders to stop himself from toppling over. Turning sharply to face the Frenchman, Duncan firmly grasped him by the wrists. 'Did you know those men would be there?' He almost snarled in anger.

'No of course not. Do you have something against Geoff, Phillippe or Patrick? Why does it matter if we were alone or with other members of the household?'

At last the mask of English stoic had fallen away as Duncan glared into François' puzzled face. 'Don't you realise that one of them could very well have killed three people this day?'

François' eyes widened, 'Surely not.' Although Duncan's fingers dug painfully into his flesh, François did not protest at the contact. He wanted to keep Duncan's focus upon the topic.

'They have the most to gain! Who else would want them dead?'

'I heard Preston ask Charles, the Footman, if there had been any news from the search of the estate for Madame Henry.' François paused slightly before he finally added, 'Duncan, mon cheri, you're hurting me.'

Horrified, the Tutor immediately released the death grip he had upon François' wrists. 'Sorry.' Duncan fell into step beside the Frenchman as he massaged his maltreated wrists.

'Revenge is a powerful motive, mon ami, but so is the desire to be Lord Whatnot.'

A grim little smile appeared on Duncan's face as he glanced across at his companion. 'Well you'd know all about that. You become Lord Whatnot in a couple of months against much family unrest. The Earl has always been very secretive about your last name, so apart from you being an Irish Lord, who exactly are you?'

Expressively spreading his hands, François shrugged his shoulders. 'I'll be a Baron like Caleb and let's stick to Lord Whatnot as I don't feel comfortable tossing recklessly around my family name.'

His eyebrows rising, Duncan asked, 'Is that how you stayed alive for this long? By denying who you really are? I mean even now you call Louise your sister rather than your mother.'

François chuckled. 'Habits can be hard to break but until I was ten and my father died, no one was remotely interested in me. From the very beginning, though, the Earl had considered how to protect us. No one was looking for a French brother and sister. It was better that we hid amongst the servants even though Monsieur Sinclair's financial wizardry and the Earl's meant that the title is no longer impoverished.'

'When my father died, the family were horrified to learn of a half French heir. When my location was revealed and instead of the streets running with my blood, Phillippe left most of them bleeding. The Earl was very, very angry, he threatened that another such attempt upon my life and he would destroy the house of… Whatnot.'

'Why the delay to claim your birthright? Surely not to protect you from your jealous relatives?'

They weaved their way slowly through the rose garden and down to the less formal woodlands.

'The Earl wanted to create something worth inheriting. He took the meagre assets to the title like a crumbling manor house, a run-down horse stud and several struggling farms as well as some of his own money and placed it all in the hands of the financial genius of Frederick Sinclair. Within five years the Earl had been paid back his initial outlay and the estate has continued to expand since as well as improve the local industry.'

'So something now worth killing for?' Duncan suggested.

François chuckled. 'Most definitely! The family have been put on a leash by the Earl though. If I die anything but a natural death before I am five and twenty, then they inherit the title only, as everything is legally the Earl's until he signs it over to me. So long as I am alive the family have a guaranteed generous allowance.'

'But once you become Lord Whatnot? What is to stop them killing you for the title and the estate?'

'The extremely clever lawyer Clive Dunn has detailed documents that if I die without issue then the family get only the title and the house, all other property is to be for Louise to dispose of as she sees fit. I have agreed to marry one of my Irish cousins, the choice of which is to be mine and she would get to live in the manor house for the rest of her life if she so wishes after my death.'

Pushing a branch out of his way Duncan chose his next words carefully. 'Won't a wife complicate your lifestyle?'

'Not in the least! I am more than capable of satisfying the needs of a wife as well as a lover. If my wife was to try and divorce me for infidelity or homosexuality, she would leave the marriage with a small allowance but the children would remain with me. I'm a fair man, mon ami, if she wishes to take a lover, I'll not stand in the way. So long as she understands that I'll tolerate no bastards!' The handsome young god's face had hardened in determination.

Beginning to realise that this was no fool who walked beside him, Duncan's next question felt inadequate. 'So a marriage of convenience? What of love? Is it only duty ahead for you?'

François shrugged. 'That is why it was decided that I got to choose from one of my many female Irish cousins rather than have one thrust upon me. You never know, I might fall madly in love with one of them and we'd live as happily ever after as Tony and Caleb should have been.'

They were back on the subject that had forced them to flee the house and Duncan sighed as he took François' hand.

'Come on! I'm sick of being serious and responsible adults.' Breaking into a run Duncan led François in a mad dash through the lush green woodlands until they finally collapsed, breathing hard, in a secluded corner of the estate. Where muted sunlight danced through the trees upon crystal clear water, an oasis from time itself.

Lizzy's Bleak Future

When Charlotte had finally fallen asleep, a weary Lizzy was at last able to leave her sister's bedroom and seek some quiet time to actually think. The trouble was that attending to Charlotte's every whim as well as a throbbing headache Lizzy wasn't certain that even if she reached the solitude of her own room she'd actually be able to imagine what the future had in store for her. *At first glance it looks rather bleak. Claude, my repellent and despised brother, yet still my brother for all that, is dead. An undeniable fact. Agnes, my over-bearing and bullying mother, yet still my mother for all that, is perhaps dead. A fact just waiting to be proved right or wrong. Even if Charlotte refuses to accept her share of our mother's pittance of a legacy, what sort of independence will it allow me?*

Trudging her way down the corridor to her own room, Lizzy sighed deeply. *There will be death duties as well as funerals for both Claude and mother, but even if they don't eat up most of that money as well as selling all of our mother's jewellery, I am keenly aware that for the last six years mother had been existing almost solely upon the allowance that Julius had made her.* Halting her footsteps, Lizzy stared unseeingly at the picture on the wall beside her. *Mother had kept a tight fist over the household budget and will have left very few debts but Claude, aside from a twisted appetite of a sexual nature, was a heavy drinker and even heavier gambler. His debts alone could break me completely and any dreams of independence would be kissed good bye. I will be forced to hang on my brother-in-law's sleeve or worse become a drudge waiting hand and foot on my sister or trying to earn my keep.*

Starting her feet moving again, Lizzy angrily wiped away the tears of shame that threatened to sweep her away on a wave of despair. *With no money, lacking my sister's good looks what hope do I have to make a decent match? Any match? Whenever Charlotte had come up to town she had taken me to all the best houses, parties and events to try and help me find a husband. Being less pretty than my sister, no dowry and the prospect of Claude and Mother as in-laws had not been helped by my acute shyness. Even when a gentleman had shown any interest in me, Mother had deemed him unsuitable.*

Pausing outside her room, Lizzy wondered, *had Mother not wanted me to marry so that she would have someone to boss around all the time?*

'Miss Lizzy?' The voice behind her made her jump but as it hadn't been said in the usual angry or judgemental tone of her mother, she didn't quake in fear as she turned and Mary closed the gap between them.

'Does Charlotte need me?' Lizzy tried to smile but tears were only moments away.

'No Miss, but have you had anything to eat since breakfast?'

Rubbing a weary hand over her eyes, Lizzy sighed. 'No, I'm not really hungry besides I have a tremendous headache.'

Mary linked her arm through Lizzy's. 'I'll give you something for your head but eating will help you. Come down to Mrs Preston's private rooms where she has some food laid out for you.'

Lizzy found she couldn't resist against the Maid as she was led downstairs to the servants domain.

'Why are you being so nice to me? I'm nobody. I couldn't possibly afford a Lady's Maid.'

Mary tut-tutted. 'Shh now! Let someone take care of you for a change. We don't have to talk but just sit quietly as you take some refreshment.'

At the solace in the Maid's voice, Lizzy's fight against crying began to crumble. 'Oh Mary, what are we going to do now? Here I've been selfishly thinking about my own problems but you must be in just as difficult a position as I am. Tony's death must be tearing your heart in two but here you are offering me comfort.' Trying to stop her tears as they flowed freely down her cheeks, Lizzy hid her face in her handkerchief as they passed curious servants.

'Hush my dear. William and I have several options for the future. Right now I can't do anything to assist Mr Bell in his pursuit to bring to justice the killers so I'm offering support to ones who most people might over look.'

Knocking upon Mrs Preston's door, Mary was a little surprised that Lizzy had broken out into heart breaking sobs. With the Housekeeper's assistance, Mary led Lizzy inside and sat her down on a sofa beneath a window in the neat parlour that was a private sanctuary for Mr and Mrs Preston. Taking Lizzy's sobbing form into her arms, Mrs Preston asked Mary to pour a glass of cordial before sitting down opposite until she had recovered.

'Nobody… nobody has ever cared how I may be feeling. I've always been the one who has to run round after everyone else!' Lizzy managed to explain, accepting a dry handkerchief to wipe her eyes and blow her nose before Mrs Preston urged her to drink.

'Even when you and her Ladyship were at home when you were younger?' motherly Mrs Preston patted Lizzy's hand.

'We always day-dreamed about how we would both escape from that house. Once one had managed to break free, they would help the other to get away.' Lizzy sobbed again.

'What went wrong?' Mary asked gently.

'Either Charlotte's ability to stand up to our mother hadn't strengthened once she got away or Mother just didn't want to lose her favourite chew toy. Now… now I'll probably drown under Claude's debts and death taxes.' Obediently Lizzy took another sip of her drink as encouraged by Mrs Preston.

'Oh but Lord Stirling won't let that happen to you Miss Lizzy!' protested Mary.

Lizzy's eyes sparkled in indignation. 'I don't want to hang on Julius' sleeve! I'm tired of being treated like a second class citizen! If I must be… be a drudge then I will find work. An elderly Lady's companion or… or a governess. Although I'm hardly qualified for the latter, Mother didn't pay too much attention to any real education for us. I'm not pretty enough to make a brilliant match like Charlotte and with no dowry why should any suitor look at me?' Before she became maudlin, Lizzy was startled out of the sad review of her shortcomings by a slap across the hand by the Housekeeper.

'Now that is enough Miss Lizzy! There's no point trying to solve any obstacles before they even present themselves. Nor is this negativity about your looks or talents at all helpful. We don't know yet if that was your mother seen running from the Manor. Now you need to stop trying to think too much, have a little something to eat, a headache powder and a rest. When you get up for dinner you may find that everything is not as bleak as you've been imaging.' Mrs Preston urged Lizzy up to the table and the selection of delicious food that she had laid out.

'Mr Dunn, his Lordship's lawyer, as well as your mother's, is still here and he should be able to give you a clearer picture of your current circumstances,' reassured Mary as Mrs Preston poured out a cup of strong tea for Lizzy while she lack-lusterly selected items from the various plates in front of her to place upon her own plate.

'I must learn to take care of myself,' sighed Lizzy as she took a sip of good strong sweetened tea.

'His Lordship won't abandon you Miss Lizzy,' reassured Mrs Preston.

'But what if something was to happen to Julius or Charlotte? I can't go on relying on other people to scrape by.'

Mary cast a quick glance across at Mrs Preston. 'Why should anything happen to Lord and Lady Stirling? They're not old or ill.'

Placing her cup back in its saucer, Lizzy picked up a triangle of sandwiches. 'Caleb, Tony and Aidan weren't old or ill either. They thought they were safe once they got back to the Manor and look where they are now!'

Mary held Mrs Preston's gaze for a speaking moment before she slipped quietly out of the room.

The Water Hole

They lay on the cool grass, slightly breathless for several minutes as it had been some time since either Duncan or François had run like that. Except for their heavy breathing, the two men were silent. Which seemed to only accentuate the natural noises around them. The gentle whisper of the breeze stirring the leaves. The call of a bird to its mate high above their heads and the occasional buzz of bees as they went from blossom to blossom, gathering pollen. In the distance they could just hear the horses out in their paddocks and the occasional bark of the Border Collie on the home farm keeping the sheep under control.

Sighing deeply at the tranquillity of their surroundings, François hauled himself to his feet and kneeling beside the water's edge bent over to splash cool water over his face. As Duncan rose on one of his elbows, François smiled mischievously and half turning, splashed water at the Tutor.

'Oy!' Duncan removed his glasses and wiped the water out of his eyes as he rose to his feet. 'I might've been angry about that if it hadn't been so refreshing.' He knelt down beside François to scoop water over his own face.

'Does it remind you of skinny dipping as a child?' François pretended to push Duncan fully clothed into the natural pool.

Grinning, Duncan grabbed François as he thought, *if I am going into the water, I'm taking the Frenchman with me!* 'Actually the last time I did it wasn't exactly that much in the distant past!' Glancing quickly around to see if there was any one around Duncan started to strip off his clothes. 'Are you game François?'

'In broad daylight? Aren't you worried about being seen?' Even so François rose to his feet to remove his own clothes.

Shrugging his shoulders out of his jacket, Duncan didn't even pause to consider the question as he ripped off his cravat. 'Do what you want to do now as tomorrow we could all be...' *I find that even in jest I cannot say "dead". It is too soon.*

Kicking off his own shoes as he quickly disrobed, François laid an understanding hand upon Duncan's shoulder. 'Last one in is a rotten egg!'

Shamelessly François stripped out of his underwear and contained a smug smile when Duncan blushed as he took in the full extent of the naked god. Not saying another word François turned and ran straight into the pool. Submerged up to his neck in the cool water, François turned to face Duncan as he stripped off the last item of clothing and followed the Frenchman into the water.

He had a perfect view of the other man's physique and wasn't displeased with the sight but François kept his hands to himself. *Firstly, I'm not positive that Duncan would welcome an advance from me, but secondly and perhaps more importantly, I've heard the sounds of someone approaching, more than one person approaching this secret oasis.*

The newcomers were too close for François and Duncan to reach their clothes before they were discovered. With his head temporarily submerged beneath the water, Duncan wasn't aware of the intrusion until he surged up out of the water to drag in a deep breath and nearly choked as on the pool's edge stood Patrick, Geoff and Phillippe.

Duncan blushed as red as a beetroot to be caught completely naked with another man. Phillippe smiled as he spread his hands expressively.

'So you two had the same idea as we did to cool down. If we are intruding we can leave again.'

'This isn't what it looks like!' Duncan hastened to state.

Both of Phillippe's eyebrows rose as he glanced around at the strewn clothing. 'It looks like two young gentlemen taking a dip. You haven't been making inappropriate suggestions to Duncan have you François?' There was a note of surprise rather than disapproval in the older Frenchman's voice.

To be frank with himself Duncan had to admit. 'Actually aside from François dragging me out of the stuffy school room, everything we have done I have suggested.' Trying to take some of the heat out of his flaming cheeks, Duncan splashed water on his face. 'Please you're all welcome to join us. Unless you'd rather we left to give you privacy?'

Phillippe glanced across at Geoff and Patrick as the former shrugged his shoulders but the latter was already reaching up to tear off his cravat.

'It does look inviting and the pool is big enough for all of us not to feel awkward,' Patrick admitted.

'Thank you Duncan, then we accept.' Phillippe joined the two Englishmen as they removed their clothes. Duncan pointedly looked away as they stripped naked but could not help casting a furtive glance as the others entered the water. François openly admired the physical attributes of the new-comers and idly wondered, *where can this communal bathe possibly lead?*

Releasing Pent Up Feelings

No one could state categorically how it had started. Even Phillippe was surprised at how easily the younger men embraced with a more childlike enthusiasm but he quickly moved out of the firing line when the others started a splashing war. The laughter that rang out over the sound of the water shooting between the young men should have been totally inappropriate for the dire events that had taken place such a short time ago. Phillippe wondered idly, *will they later regret this moment of merriment or is this what they really needed to cope with such a monumental loss?*

What it most certainly meant was that none of them heard the approach of a strolling couple who had been attracted by all the noise the bathers had been making. It was not until Andre and Rosemary had stopped at the edge of the pool that any of the younger men were aware of their presence.

Realising that a lady was present, Duncan stopped splashing and copped a face full of water from Geoff. As the others realised that they were not alone, the splashing ceased which only increased their embarrassment. The movement of the water had been a natural barrier for their modesty. By allowing the crystal clear water to settle down, they revealed the extent of their nakedness. When Rosemary giggled, Andre turned her to face in the opposite direction as several of the gentlemen in the water turned bright red and attempted to cover up their genitalia.

'Well,' one of Andre's eyebrows rose. 'Rosemary was wondering if Delacourt had found some way to relieve his stress but it would seem that he'd found some like-minded companions.' There was no judgement or condemnation in the Author's voice so although the young men were still embarrassed, they weren't insulted or defensive. A chuckle came from Phillippe who unlike his younger companions wasn't struck dumb by the presence of a Lady.

'I'm afraid that the instruction of the sensuality of the art of fencing left my young pupils a little hot under the collar.'

His old friend groaned in disbelief. 'Not that old chestnut!' said Andre, 'I never really understood it the first time you tried to explain your hidden messages.'

A mischievous smile appeared on Phillippe's face as one of his own eye brows rose slowly. 'But then I failed to manage to teach your two left feet to dance!' He drawled sarcastically but Andre only laughed.

'That's because whenever you said "left" you meant your left and visa versa! So how did your pupils fare? Did you confuse them completely so that they no longer know if they were supposed to dance, make love or fight a duel?'

Sweeping his hand towards Patrick and Geoff, Phillippe admitted, 'I did confuse them so I suggested instead that we should cool off.'

Rosemary stood on her tippy toes to whisper into Andre's ear and he nodded.

'An excellent idea, ma cherie. Rosemary asked if you'd like us to send some towels down to you.' Andre placed his arm around Rosemary's waist.

'That is an appreciative offer but Andre...' Phillippe paused mischievously as Andre glanced back at him.

'Oui?'

'Better make certain that a male servant brings them down.' The Englishmen's blushes deepened and Andre laughed as he led Rosemary back towards the Manor.

Bell's Team Assembles

Preston, the Butler, having appeared in the entrance hall because Bell had called him by name as he entered through the front doors was more than a little stunned to find four people descend upon him from different directions. Not that even a hint of emotion disturbed his professional demur and aplomb.

'Where is his Lordship?' asked Bell, dragging off his hat and coat. Taking the outer garments to hang up Preston answered.

'Lord Stirling is in Lord Caleb's room.'

'Are Lady and Lord Stirling in danger?' demanded Mary before Rosemary or Andre could speak. Preston held up his hand for silence and indicated that the others should follow him out of the entrance hall

'Come to Lord Stirling's study, we may speak freely then.'

Obediently, his companions remained silent until Preston had closed the study door behind their entrance.

'I just took tea up to his Lordship, having made it myself and he locked the door behind me,' Preston finally answered Mary's anguished question.

Nodding, Bell added, 'One of my people is keeping an eye on Lady Charlotte.'

Screwing up her pretty nose, Rosemary looked a little puzzled. 'Wouldn't it be a little reckless to kill Lord and Lady Stirling with all eyes focussed squarely on the Manor due to this morning's murders?'

'Unless,' Andre stroked his chin in thought, 'they intended Madame Henry to be the scapegoat for all murders.'

Striding across to the French windows to ensure they were properly closed, Bell stated, 'Well they should have arranged for Agnes Henry to be killed at a later time or that she shouldn't have been discovered so soon.'

Bell turned back to face the others. 'Doctor Masters has confirmed that the body in the barn is Agnes Henry. Whether or not he'll be able to tell us how much time had elapsed before Solitaire found her may be impossible even after an autopsy.'

'But we can be assured that Madame Henry can have nothing to do with anything that may or may not happen in the future to Lord or Lady Stirling.' Andre concluded, gallantly indicating that Mary and Rosemary should be seated in the two arm chairs as he perched on the edge of the Earl's desk.

Drawing his fob watch out of his pocket, Bell nodded, slightly distracted. 'Where currently are our four main suspects?'

'Lizzy is having something to eat with Mrs Preston but she would like to go to her room to lie down,' Mary reported.

Bell nodded. 'Just give me a five minute head start before you go back to Miss Henry so that I can make certain my man has left no trace of his search of her room.'

Swinging one booted leg, Andre stated, 'Geoff, Patrick and Duncan are down at the watering hole with Phillippe and François. I'm to send towels out for them.

Bell glanced down at his watch again. 'Don't be in any hurry to get back to them, Monsieur Guillaume, but don't be so long that they realise we're deliberately keeping them out of the way. I'm about to check that all my men have finished their search of the Manor.'

Clearing his throat and holding up his hand for silence, Preston had heard footsteps out in the corridor and both ladies inside the study jumped when the footsteps halted outside the room and a knock came upon the door. The Butler looked at

Bell and didn't move to open the door until the Bow Street Runner had nodded his head. As Lady Margarette stepped over the threshold, Andre slipped off the edge of the desk and along with the two other men, bowed as the two women hastily rose to their feet and curtsied. The Dowager Countess acknowledged this respect with a slight inclination of her head.

'No one else seems to give me a straight answer, so Preston I'm hoping you can tell me where is my son?' There was no anger in the elderly woman's calm voice but more than a hint of aspiration.

'The Earl is in Lord Caleb's room, my Lady,' answered the Butler.

Her eyebrows rose in surprise, Lady Margarette transferred her gaze to Mary. 'Is that a sensible place for my son to be, Mary? I thought Doctor Masters would have taken…' There was a sudden catch in the Dowager Countess' voice that she shrugged to overcome. 'Taken away the bodies of my grandchildren by now.'

Mary bobbed another curtsy. 'It's probably the safest place for his Lordship at the moment, my Lady.'

'Safest?' Lady Margarette turned her penetrating gaze upon Bell. 'Mr Bell are you any nearer a solution? What danger does this household still stand in?'

Glancing down at his watch once more, Bell finally slipped it back into the pocket of his waistcoat. 'I need to review all the evidence that my men have just collected, my Lady, but I hope to be able to be present to you and Lord Stirling your grandchildren's killers within the next hour.'

As Rosemary and Mary gasped in shock, Andre's head swung round to stare at the detective. 'You know then who is behind all this?' demanded the Author.

'I have my suspicions but it will be the evidence that will prove it for everyone's satisfaction.'

A deep sigh from the Dowager Countess surprised them all. 'The only way I'll be completely satisfied, Mr Bell, is if there was some way you knew how to turn back the hands of time but if all I'm allowed is to see my grandchildren's killer hang for their murder then so be it.' As the elderly Lady turned back to the door, Bell stepped forward.

'May I escort you back to your room, Lady Stirling?'

'Thank you but no, you have a lot of work to do if you intend to meet your deadline Mr Bell.'

Once again, those assembled bowed or curtsied as the Dowager Countess left the room.

'Are there any other questions?' Bell asked his assistants. There was a general shaking of heads.

'Mr Preston, I'm hoping that a gentleman from London will arrive before I have to address the family with my solution. I would prefer it if no one else in the household was aware of this man's presence until I deem it necessary.'

Preston inclined his head. 'I'll escort the gentleman to Mrs Preston's sitting room until you're ready for him.'

Bell double-checked that he had his notebook as well as a variety of other papers, most significantly, Tony's account of their adventures up until their safe arrival back at the Manor.

'Thank you, we only need to maintain our silence for a little longer.' Bell indicated that their meeting was over and they left the study, each with their own tasks to perform.

Bell Lays Out His Investigation

It was closer to two hours later that Officer Bell finally called all members of the household together in the morning room. With the exception of Mary, William and the Prestons, the rest of the servants weren't included as they would be busy preparing for dinner and Mr Preston had promised that the moment they knew the identity of the murderer, he would inform all below stairs. François led a rather hesitant Louise and Rosemary to their chairs as they were uncertain if they should actually be there.

Phillippe looked after Lady Margarette and his mother, Monique while Andre seated Isabella, Charlotte and Lizzy. Patience Sinclair entered the room, leaning on her husband's arm and although she was no longer crying, the handkerchief she raised to reddened eyes was a crumpled damp version of its former self.

The men positioned themselves towards the back of the room along with Patrick, Geoff and Duncan. The Tutor was a little surprised to see his parents walk through the door but leaning towards him, Phillippe explained.

'Monsieur Bell thought that your parents would be a comfort and moral support during this family's dire time of need.'

Satisfied, Duncan nodded and continued to watch the procession as family and friends gathered for the final piece of the puzzle.

A nondescript little middled aged man entered the morning room with the Earl and both men paused to speak to Officer Abraham Bell. 'Thank you for coming at such short notice, Sir,' said Bell, shaking the little man's hand. 'Was I correct?'

The little man nodded. 'Yes.'

Bell breathed a sigh of relief. 'I'm sorry for that but it does mean it all makes sense.'

Sympathetically, the little man patted Bell's arm before joining Clive Dunn, the Earl's lawyer on chairs slightly apart from the family. The Earl sat down beside his mother and laid his hand over hers as Doctor Masters closed the door behind him and nodded to Bell to indicate that he had completed his assigned task.

The Moreau brothers were guarding the exits of the drawing room so that if the killer tried to escape before or after his or her identity was revealed, they wouldn't get far.

As all eyes in the room turned to rest upon Bell while he sorted his numerous papers on the table on front of him, he cleared his throat and finally looked up.

'Ladies and gentlemen, we are faced with the fact that in this room is one or more than one murderer. Several people benefit from the death of each of the victims. Lord Caleb leaves several legacies to various servants, an allowance for life for his mother, but the title and estate go to his cousin Geoff.' Glancing briefly around the room Bell continued, 'Lady Antonia left several legacies to various servants and villagers but the bulk of her assets have been left to Heather Gray for her charity work with women and girls.' Bell paused for protests and he was not to be disappointed. Although it wasn't the person he had expected to raise a protest.

'Surely Tony's dowry was transferred to her husband upon signing their marriage certificates?' queried Lizzy.

A chuckle came from Doctor Masters. 'Not if you're the daughter of an Earl, the granddaughter of a financial wizard or have very clever lawyers,' he drawled.

Clive Dunn flushed at such high praise, as one so used to being maligned in his profession. A gentle smile touched the Earl's lips. 'Caleb agreed that Tony should have complete control over her own inheritance. She... she had plans to use it to improve the future for any other sons aside from the eldest they may have had and to ensure an independence for any daughters.' The Earl released his mother's hand to draw a handkerchief out of his trouser pocket and handed it to Isabella who had uttered a sob as she tried to contain her tears. The image of the grandchildren that she would never see was too much for Isabella's struggle against breaking down completely.

'My apologies, Lady Isabella,' Bell stated, 'this is going to be painful for all of you but I felt you needed to know the why and how this tragedy had happened and not just the who.'

Dragging in a deep, shuddering breath, Isabella dabbed at her eyes with the Earls' handkerchief and accepted the glass of cordial that Frederick Sinclair, seated closest to her, placed into her hand.

'Go on Mr Bell, I suppose we'll all be blubbering by the end but you're right, we need to know the whole truth.'

Taking a deep breath Bell let it out slowly as his eyes scanned all the faces in the room before he finally began to explain. 'More than one person in this room benefits from the recent deaths of five people but was this the work of one suspect and the other deaths were collateral damage or coincidences or are more than one suspects working together to meet mutual goals? I've ruled out the servants and the local villagers.'

Bell was interrupted at that moment by Patrick, 'Why?'

'Because none of them knew that Lady Antonia had even made a will, let alone left them anything in it,' explained Clive Dunn.

'Surely someone had to witness the wills, they could've let slip about the expected windfall,' argued Patrick.

The lawyer looked superciliously at the young man over the top of his pincer glasses. 'The witnesses were Lady Antonia's grandparents, Mr and Mrs Sinclair as they were not named in the will. They had no reason to inform anyone of the will's content.'

Bell nodded.' Thank you Mr Dunn. I have also ruled out the French visitors and relatives. If they had any serious dispute with the victims then they had ample opportunity to kill them in Paris. So that leaves us with a very small pool of possible candidates.' Pausing, the Bow Street Runner sorted through some of the papers in front of him. The room was in absolute silence as they waited in nervous expectancy for Bell to pull his rabbit out of his hat.

Agnes Henry

'Agnes Henry was a lot of things but the one thing she was not was a fool. I can easily imagine she wanted revenge on Lord Caleb for her son's death, wanted to humiliate Lady Antonia for her treatment while in this house, or hurt Lord Stirling for threatening to cut Agnes and Claude off financially but I do not see her putting her chance to have a Henry heir to the Stirling title at risk by insisting that Nigel Sutherland take Lord Aidan during the second abduction.'

'But Adam kept the letter of instruction signed by Agnes,' stated William, surprising himself for speaking up but he had actually seen the letter the dying Adam had given Officer Bell.

'Yes William, now I've had an opportunity to compare old letters of Mrs Henry's with the instruction letter and although I'm not a handwriting expert I feel positive claiming that Adam's letter was a forgery. A very clever forgery but a forgery nevertheless.'

'But Claude turned up in Paris to kidnap Aidan and bring him home. Wasn't that all part of the original second abduction plan?' asked Geoff.

Bell shook his head. 'The second letter of instructions said to kill all three of the victims. The writer couldn't guarantee that the victims would be able to escape before Claude reached the French shore. Even though Lady Charlotte is pregnant again, Agnes couldn't guarantee that her daughter would bear another son. She would not jeopardise the heir that already lived which is when she sent Claude to Paris after hearing of the second abduction to bring just Lord Aidan home.'

Deep in contemplation, Frederick Sinclair stroked his chin. 'Even though Agnes was seen in the vicinity of the Manor today, you don't believe she is responsible for poisoning my grandchildren for that same reason? She wouldn't risk losing Aidan.'

Bell nodded. 'In part yes, Mr Sinclair, but there are a couple of other reasons. The servant who saw her said she was running away from the Manor. Firstly by running instead of walking, the woman drew attention to herself deliberately, secondly Mrs Henry wasn't the sort of woman who naturally ran. Thirdly, no one actually saw her inside the house. Lastly, when the Patterson brothers found her in the barn, Mrs Henry had been dead possibly at least half an hour before the running figure had even been seen outside the Manor.'

Charlotte wore a perplexed frown as she tried to understand what the officer of the law was trying to tell them. 'So someone murdered Mama, then dressed up as her intending that she took the blame for the poisonings?'

'Yes Lady Charlotte,' agreed Bell.

'That's horrible!' she declared, and there followed a slightly awkward silence as, although everyone else in the room abhorred violence, no one was actually upset by the passing of Agnes Henry.

Patrick Stirling

Clearing his throat, Bell refocused the attention of the room back to him. 'Patrick Stirling, you were annoyed by your cousin encouraging the Earl to marry again to produce a direct heir and you hated the way Lord Caleb had, to put it in your own words, "taken the place in Lady Antonia's heart that you wished could have been yours". You could easily have laid your hands on old letters from Agnes Henry or convinced her to journey down here when you left London this morning.'

'You had the opportunity to poison the cordial when you went upstairs to change, you did not go immediately to the church which gave you ample time to murder Mrs Henry, dress up as her and make sure you were seen before eventually turning up in time for the wedding.'

Something akin to a sneer appeared on Patrick's face as he said, 'Prove it!'

Geoff Delacourt

Not accepting the challenge, Bell turned his attention to the next suspect. 'Geoff Delacourt, you stand to inherit your cousin's title, his property and can comfort your charming Aunt Isabella, who is as loving and caring as your mother was not. You didn't come downstairs with Lord Caleb which gave you the opportunity to poison the cordials, you were seen outside the church smoking a cigar but no one can account for your whole time outside. It is a short distance from the village to the barn where Mrs Henry's body was found.'

'You were given free range of the Manor after the first abduction and could easily have found letters of Mrs Henry's to copy for the instructions. Until you and your cousin came to Stirling, your position as his heir seemed assured but once Lord Caleb took that definite step towards matrimony and a family he and his new wife needed to be removed.'

Although Geoff flushed a deep crimson, he managed to say quite calmly. 'It does sound damning when you explain it like that.'

Lizzy Henry

'Lizzy Henry, you had extremely strong incentives to murder two of the victims,' Bell turning to Lizzy had made her jump in surprise.

'Me? I had nothing against Caleb, Tony or Aidan!' She squeaked in protest.

'No, I meant your mother and your brother,' Bell clarified and when he received a guilty little 'Oh!' he then continued to speak.

'You hated both Agnes and Claude with every fibre of your being. For what they made you do, for the life they refused to let you have away from them and for all the insults, bullying and demeaning acts and words. If you were going to succeed in achieving any sort of freedom you needed them out of your life permanently. Lady Charlotte had escaped and yet your mother still pulled the strings.'

'"Lotte is the pretty one, we'll find a rich and titled husband for her and sponge off them forever. Poor Lizzy, she always was an ugly child, I didn't suppose I'll ever get her off my hands but at least I have my darling Claude to depend upon."' Bell's imitation of Agnes Henry was so accurate that Charlotte gasped in surprise and Lizzy flushed up to her ears. Her hands tightened into two angry little fists. *So many times I had heard those or similar words as Mother had discussed her children with her friends.*

'Caleb shot Claude and that was an accident. I had no reason to hurt Caleb, Tony or Aidan.' Lizzy was unsuccessful in keeping a tremor out of her voice.

'You had a good reason for hating your sister. All those promises you had both made when you were young. How both of you were going to escape that house. For six years your sister has been free so where was your freedom? Oh Lady Charlotte took you to several parties and other functions, introduced you to eligible men but nothing ever came of it. Were they not eligible enough for Agnes or did she like keeping you as her personal slave, belittling you because you couldn't get a husband when she was the reason you were still stuck in that house of horror?'

'Why wasn't Lady Charlotte, supposedly now free from her mother's influence, strong enough to stand up to Agnes' tyranny? She could have insisted that your mother let you marry. She could have asked you to come and live here at the Manor. She could have told the Earl what you were being subjected to by your brother. Lady Charlotte was surprised when you revealed that you too had to service Claude's voracious sexual appetite. Why? Did she think that the money supplied by the Earl was enough to satisfy Claude's perversion somewhere else or did she think you were too ugly for your brother to be bothered with? You could even hate your sister enough to want to take everything that she has away from Charlotte. Her son, her husband, her life!'

Although Charlotte didn't actually move away from her sister, she did raise tear-filled, puzzled eyes up to meet Lizzy's.

'Lizzy?' There were a hundred and one question in that one word.

'What would I gain from killing my sister and brother-in-law?' Lizzy demanded of Bell. 'How could I possibly survive without them?'

Bell wasn't put out by Lizzy's attack. 'That would depend if you had become aware that the Earl intended to settle an income and property upon you.'

All the colour drained form Lizzy's face as she glanced across at Earl Stirling. 'What? You put me into your will?'

'No Lizzy, I was going to give you your independence now,' her brother-in-law explained.

'I didn't know.' Lizzy's voice quavered.

Bell brought their attention back to him. 'Or were you hoping for higher rewards Miss Henry? If you were working with someone else who could perhaps make you Lady Delacourt or Lady Stirling? Was this a team effort to ensure that the three of you got what you all desired most?'

Lizzy looked like she was about to burst into tears. Geoff sat with compressed lips and folded arms. Patrick glanced around the room as if gauging the accessibility of the various means of escape.

A Final Suspect Is Revealed

'Or have all three of you been played by a very manipulative and skilful puppet master? Are you just pawns being moved masterfully upon a chess board? Pawns whose motives for the victims' murders are so blatantly obvious that we wouldn't even look for the chess master's motive. He loved Lady Antonia. He knew that his future way of life wasn't suitable for her. So why on earth would Duncan Gray possibly want her dead?' At Bell's words, all heads turned around to look at the Tutor, who appeared amused as he raised one sardonic eyebrow.

'I presume that is a rhetorical question and you're going to dazzle us with a preposterous reason for all this carnage.'

Breaking eye contact with Duncan, Bell looked down at the table in front of him and deliberately took his time in sorting the papers into several different piles.

'Did you really think no one would ever figure it out Mr Gray? That your vast intellect made you unbeatable in this game of chess?' Slowly Bell raised his eyes again to rest upon Duncan as one of his fingers gently tapped upon the pile of papers directly in front of him.

'You are out of your league little man! But give it your best shot.' Duncan wasn't in the least disturbed by the finger that continued to tap the papers.

'All of this, the second abduction, the dropping them in enemy territory and finally poisoning them, was just because you made a mistake. The great intellect of Duncan Gray made the simple mistake of not locking a door.'

'Mr Bell,' Reverend Gray had risen to his feet. 'I do not appreciate this slanderous attack upon my son!'

'It's all right Pop, the man's on a fishing expedition. If he had any real proof he wouldn't be trying to frighten us into a rash confession.' Duncan sneered at Bell as his father resumed his seat, 'Go on, what mistake did I make that has led to the deaths of five people? Six if you include Adam. What door did I presumably leave open?'

Not immediately answering, the Bow Street Runner lifted up one of the piles of papers and scanned through them leisurely until he found the section he wanted.

'After the first abduction when Lord Caleb had asked Lady Antonia to marry him, she came up to the school room to tell you privately of their engagement.'

Bell was interrupted by the Earl. 'Why did Tony want to tell Duncan separately that she had agreed to marry Caleb? Had Duncan made inappropriate advances upon my daughter?'

Bell briefly nodded. 'After the attack upon Lady Antonia as they left the Stirling Arms Inn, Mr Gray dressed her Ladyship's swollen ankle and when their conversation turned to the future, he kissed her. Mr Gray admitted he was in love with Lady Antonia but knew he was heading for London, maybe the Continent and that world was not suitable for her Ladyship.'

Both of Duncan's eyebrows rose this time. 'You seem to have a very good idea about what happened that night. Surely all this detail wasn't in Tony's account of the abductions?'

Bell inclined his head slightly. 'Her Ladyship has given me a very, very detailed report on everything that happened since that first night when you all walked into the Stirling Arms Inn.' There was a deliberate pause as Bell locked his eyes with Duncan's before slowly repeating, 'Everything!'

As a flush ran across Duncan's cheeks, Andre sat up a little straighter. 'You don't mean every little detail do you? Forgive me ladies but I mean what Tony and Caleb got up to when they were naughty,' asked the Author.

A little flushed himself, Bell hastened to reassure. 'No, Monsieur Guillaume, no intimate details were necessary.'

The Earl put them swiftly back on track as he did not want to think about his baby girl being sexually active. 'You were

155

saying, Mr Bell, that Tony went up to the school room to talk privately with Duncan after Caleb had asked her to marry him.'

'Thank you Lord Stirling,' Bell gratefully returned to the important topic. 'Lady Antonia knocked on the school room door and called out but when you didn't answer she entered the room. You were so deep in concentration that you didn't even know that Lady Antonia was standing right beside you, let alone in the room.'

'At a glance her Ladyship was able to see that you weren't working on personal correspondence or Lord Aidan's school work so that just left some top secret government business and she drew your attention to her presence.'

Deliberately yawning, Duncan looked extremely bored. 'If this is how you tell your children bedtime stories then they must drop off in a matter of minutes,' he drawled.

'Please stay with me Mr Gray, I'm getting to the relevant part.'

Duncan shrugged his shoulders as he deliberately yawned again but his mother was watching him with a puzzled expression on her face.

'As you turned over what you'd been working on, her Ladyship said that if the government already had you working on top secret documents that you should lock the door. Now you had a problem. I believe that Lady Antonia is not the sort of Lady to read someone else's mail but she may have seen something that she should not have. She might not immediately realise the significance of what she had read but when your plans were put into action, Lady Antonia could remember what she had inadvertently seen. You couldn't afford to let Lady Antonia tell anyone what you've been up to.'

In indignation, Lady Margarette stiffened. 'Are you saying, Mr Bell, that my granddaughter would betray her own country?'

'No, my Lady, in fact the opposite,' Bell hastened to reassure. 'These aren't documents sent by our government for you to analyse now are they Mr Gray?' Bell held up one handful of papers, prepared to let Duncan see them but refused to let them out of his grasp.

'You have no way of proving that, Mr Bell.' Duncan leant back in his chair but sweat had begun to bead slightly over his top lip.

'Do you recognise this man?' Bell indicated to the dapper little middle aged gentleman who was sitting beside Clive Dunn.

'No, should I?'

'I'm not surprised as Sir Laurence Bishop has made it his ambition to be unseen. He works in the same foreign affairs department of the government that you were planning to join when you went up to London. All information that enters that department passes before Sir Laurence first.'

Duncan had gone very still. 'Are you telling me that one man, any man could remember every single document that crosses his desk? It's not possible!'

'Actually it is. Sir Laurence has what is called an identic memory. The documents in your possession have never been seen by anyone else in our government.'

There was a gasp from several of the people present but Duncan was completely focussed upon the Bow Street Runner. 'I could have acquired those documents through other channels and have been analysing their authenticity before I sent them up to London.' Duncan countered.

'Considering the time sensitivity and highly volatile nature of these letters surely you would've sent some word to the Foreign Office about what you had in your possession?'

Duncan's eyebrows rose in mock surprise. 'There are four different languages there, Mr Bell, have you really translated all of them in the short time I was lured out of my room?'

A slight smile appeared on Bell's features as he held up a second stack of papers. 'That's not all I've had translated!' He let

Duncan have a closer look at the papers in his hand and was satisfied when the Tutor's face drained of all colour.

'You're lying! It would take weeks, if not months, for an expert code breaker to crack my personal notes!' Some of the colour returned to his face as Duncan realised that Bell must be bluffing.

'That is also why you had to murder Lady Antonia isn't it? She was the only other person alive who knew your code. So if your plans failed and you weren't able to get to your notes in time, she could reveal just how you masterminded the whole plot to bring down England!'

There was another collection of gasps within the room but Duncan had blanked them all out, even the horror of his own parents. 'Now you're making things up Bell, unless Tony had written down somewhere how to read my code, you have no way of saying with confidence what my notes are really about.'

Putting down the handful of coded notes Bell picked up another selection of papers. 'I won't bore you with reading the whole translation but apart from describing how you manipulated your pawns to do your dirty work, shall I just give you the highlights of your treasonous plot?' Receiving no answer, Bell continued, 'Let's start with the letters – they are from England's allies in defeating Napoleon at Waterloo. It is regarding terms for transferring their allegiance to France once your plot to destabilise the English government and rescue Napoleon from his prison on St Helena Island has succeeded.'

'There are also your deals with the government in the American colonies to keep the best of England's troops engaged over there in conflict. You have a contract with Lord François' family in Ireland that states you'll deliver his Lordship with his whole inheritance to them if they will start a revolt that will require the English government to send troops across to Ireland to contain it.'

'Oh and what about your plans closer to home? The Guy Fawkes style plot to blow up parliament or, my personal favourite, the replacing the German King Georges of Hanover with a Scottish Prince, so England will be leaderless and friendless when Napoleon is released from prison. How's that for a summary, Mr Gray? Have I left out anything of critical detail from your coded plans?'

There was an absolute, deafening silence as everyone stared dumbfounded at Duncan. He had eyes only for Bell as he dragged in deep breaths trying to maintain control over his temper.

'You devil!' Duncan exploded out of his chair and had grasped Bell by the lapels of his jacket before anyone else could react. 'How? I killed the woman I love so that no one would be able to stop my plans for absolute power! There is no way in hell that you broke my code! How has this happened? I factored in every possible action and reaction of each key player!' His admission of guilt caused the occupants of the room to erupt into noise and activity. Andre and François dragged Duncan back from the Bow Street Runner whereas Phillippe had to restrain the Earl as he leapt out of his seat reaching for Duncan's throat.

'You murdered my children! You were supposed to be their friend!' The Earl's hands never reached Duncan but Phillippe needed William to assist him in keeping Earl Stirling from breaking free of his hold.

With cold deliberation Lady Margarette rose to her feet and moving calmly around the milling people and Bell's table, her Ladyship took down one of the broad swords that hung decoratively over the fireplace. Making her way back to stand beside Duncan, Lady Margarette raised the broad sword high in the air, ready to strike down the cause of the death of her grandchildren.

Bell's Final Ace Card

'Grandmama! No!' A familiar, beloved voice, one she had never thought to ever hear again, commanded from the doorway. Lady Margarette froze with the sword still in the air, as she and everyone else in the morning room turned towards the open door. Looking the picture of excellent health stood Tony, Caleb and Aidan, in his brother-in-law's arms. A stunned silence fell over the room as Tony, no longer wearing her wedding dress but attired once more in one of Charlotte's altered dresses, moved through the frozen room to take the sword out of her grandmother's hands.

Aside from the dressing over the bullet graze to the side of Caleb's head and wearing the dark glasses supplied by Doctor Masters, Caleb and Aidan had also changed out of the wedding attire and back into normal clothes.

'It's over now!' Tony led the Dowager Countess back to her chair and those assembled burst into speech, all at the same time. It was an explosion of words.

Forcefully grabbing Tony by the shoulders, Duncan screamed, 'No! This isn't real! It's not possible that I miscalculated any opponent's move!' He shook Tony like a rag doll but Duncan forgot that not that long ago she was Lord Tony. Or the fact that she now held the broad sword. She stomped hard on Duncan's foot and when he released her arms, thrust her knee into his groin and as he doubled over in pain, raised the sword up over her head just like her grandmother had done only minutes earlier. Before Tony could strike a fatal blow, Caleb, lowering Aidan to the ground, grabbed Duncan by the shoulders, spun him around and floored him with a wicked right hook.

Taking the sword away from Tony, the Bow Street Runner raised his voice over all the noise. 'Ladies and Gentlemen! Ladies and Gentlemen!' He repeated when the noise level had begun to subside. 'Please resume your seats and all will be explained.' Not another word did Bell say as those standing returned to their previous positions but he could not immediately continue.

Keeping Aidan by his side, Caleb knelt down in front of his mother as she wept in relief and Lizzy had her hands full as Charlotte had fainted at the sight of her supposedly dead son come back to life so abruptly. Smelling salts brought Charlotte round but meant Lizzy had to now deal with her sister's hysterical sobs. Before it led to Charlotte being physically sick, Lizzy slapped her across the face. The sobs broke off in a whimper but although Charlotte continued to cry, it was less violent.

While they waited for quiet so Bell could explain, Tony knelt down in front of her grandmothers, Lady Margarette and Patience Sinclair and placed a hand over each of theirs. Patience was crying softly, in relief and clung to Tony's hand.

'I'm sorry but it was absolutely necessary that it seemed that whoever was out to kill us had finally won,' explained Tony.

'Why?' Lady Margarette's question included not just her granddaughter but Bell as well.

'Lady Antonia, Lord Caleb, if you could be seated, I'll explain.' Bell directed the newlyweds to an empty couple of chairs and Aidan sat upon Caleb's knee. 'Each time Lady Antonia and Lord Caleb managed to foil the attempts to dispose of them, it meant that there would be another attempt and then another. By pretending that the poisoning attempt had succeeded, it meant the killers could finally relax. Their job was done and their defences would be lowered.'

'I needed time to examine each suspect as well as search the house for evidence against my prime suspects. With everyone thinking they were already dead, no one would continue to try to kill them. We just had to limit the number of people who knew the truth and get the suspects out of the house so that my men could search their rooms.'

Duncan sat in his chair, nursing his injured jaw where Caleb had hit him. 'I don't understand, how did you know about the poison in advance? What did I do wrong? What miscalculation did I make?'

'When Mr Preston heard about Agnes Henry running away from the Manor, he went upstairs to see if anything was out of order in Lord Caleb's and Lady Antonia's rooms. Mr Preston is the one who makes the cordials for the household so when he detected the odour of burnt almonds he knew that something was amiss. Cyanide is colourless and tasteless but not odourless and Mr Preston knows without a doubt what the cordials should smell like. When the newlyweds returned to the house, Mr Preston discussed his concerns with Lord Caleb and he sent one of the Grooms down to the church to catch me before I took the Doyle brothers up to London.'

'All right!' interrupted Duncan. 'Detecting poison in the cordial jugs in Caleb's room would have pointed you in the direction of Agnes, or if you didn't buy her involvement, Lizzy, Geoff or Patrick. Until you had my notes and Tony had translated them, how could you have known I had anything to do with it?'

Bell held up Duncan's notes. 'You clearly outlined the actions and reactions of all your key players but you forgot a couple of minor characters. Agnes Henry was never meant to be discovered so quickly by the arrival of the Patterson brothers. It should have been more difficult for the Doctor to accurately pin point her time of death.'

'That does not explain,' sneered Duncan, 'how you discovered my involvement.'

'When I asked for a list of suspects once we had ruled out Agnes Henry that left us with Lizzy, Geoff and Patrick as our top contenders. I was about to verify Agnes's body when Doctor Masters asked if you were a suspect.'

'Why?' Duncan demanded, 'Old Masters has never liked me!'

'There seemed no deliberate bias against you, Mr Gray. Simply the fact that you were in love with Lady Antonia. In defending you, the Earl mentioned how you were doing important work for our government and about your superior intellect.'

Duncan could not help smirking. 'Well?'

'Patience isn't in your vocabulary is it, son?' drawled Bell. 'The Doctor raised the question that if you're so intelligent how come you lose to the Earl in chess? His Lordship's answer was that you were probably humouring him.'

'Is that all you had?' Duncan burst out laughing. 'The fact I let my boss win a silly board game?'

'Not silly, son, it showed me a glimpse into your mind. How you could manipulate people without them really knowing you're pulling their strings. It was no more than an idea, it seemed preposterous with three serious suspects but I needed to be sure. So I sent a message to London to find out if you were in fact working on something for the Foreign Office, something our government was involved with, but it didn't explain why Lady Antonia should be killed. So I asked her Ladyship to go into as much detail as she could remember of the incident.'

Duncan snorted. 'She had her head full of her engagement news! I doubt she could've seen past the stars in her eyes!'

'Blind to her surroundings? Oh you'd like that Mr Gray, but I'm afraid Lady Antonia was paying more attention than you realised,' Bell singled out one piece of paper from his mountain of notes. 'The top letter was in French, the one beside it, in Russian but it was your personal code that had me intrigued. If you communicated using code with London then they would have the key to unlocking the code. Sir Laurence confirmed that it was unknown to them.'

'You got lucky!' snarled Duncan.

Bell shook his head. 'No Mr Gray, you got sloppy!' Clearing his throat the Officer continued to explain to everyone in the room.

'I knew we couldn't keep up the facade that Lord Caleb, Lord Aidan and Lady Antonia were supposedly dead for longer than one day but I needed the time to build my case.'

Lady Margarette nodded. 'Well? Do you have the evidence to who is actually involved?'

'Yes, my Lady.' Bell bowed slightly. 'Duncan Gray's notes, a dress from Lizzy Henry's bedroom, splattered with her mother's blood, remnants of a burnt wig and dress in Patrick Stirling's room where he had tried to burn the evidence of impersonating Agnes Henry. The bottle of poison had been thrown out of Lord Caleb's window and smashed upon contact with the ground but when they opened the window, the poisoner accidently cut themselves on the windowsill.'

Before she could stop herself, Lizzy self-consciously pulled down the sleeves of her dress to cover her wrists. Duncan sighed as the action had betrayed Lizzy's guilt.

'You didn't need to bluff us into revealing who administered the poison Mr Bell,' said Duncan. 'You already have my notes so you know that although Patrick wants to remove Aidan and the Earl to achieve the title, he doesn't have the stomach to kill Tony so I had to rely upon Lizzy's bitterness to get the job done. Geoff Delacourt was a lost cause as he honestly does not want his cousin's title or property.'

Growing red around the ears, Geoff shrugged sheepishly. 'I didn't want to be my cousin, I just wanted to be with him,' he admitted.

Geoff's Experiment

Glancing down at Tony, when she smiled and nodded, Caleb transferred Aidan to his sister's lap and rose to his feet.

Surprising everyone in the room, Caleb drew his cousin up onto his feet and kissed him. On the mouth. Passionately. It wasn't harsh or demanding or even domineering but it caused a gasp to arise around the room as it was tender, loving and enticing. When Caleb drew back, Geoff wore a puzzled expression but didn't say anything immediately. Staring at his cousin for a moment, Geoff was obviously analysing what had just happened.

Making a decision, Geoff stepped around Caleb and sitting down beside Tony and ignoring the protests of her family, he drew her into his arms to kiss her. Tony didn't fight against Geoff's possession but responded, a little more shyly than if it had been Caleb. Satisfied with his experiment, Geoff released Tony and standing up, faced his cousin.

'I think I love being in your company rather than wanting to make love to you,' Geoff admitted.

Caleb laughed. 'Good, I'm glad cousin. I don't think I could do that again if it hadn't been for Phillippe suggesting you needed to clarify what you actually wanted.'

Well That Seems All Very Clear

Regally Lady Margarette rose to her feet. 'Well if that intimate demonstration brings an end to this session of revelations, I suggest Mr Bell takes away Duncan, Lizzy and Patrick and we can perhaps dress for dinner.' Her Ladyship reached out her hand to Tony who rose, still holding Aidan's hand and hugged their grandmother.

'I'm relieved beyond words, my darling girl, that you're not dead but I pray that we never have to go through a day like today ever again!'

Aidan looked up into his grandmother's face. 'Not even the wedding bit Grandmama?'

Lady Margarette caressed his cheek. 'Only if it doesn't include the Doyle brothers bursting into the church.'

Geoff offered his arm to the Dowager Countess to lead her up to her room as Tony, Aidan and Caleb received hugs and kisses from relieved relatives. Bell bundled together all his paperwork and tied it up with string before he and his men who had been waiting outside, escorted the conspirators out to an awaiting carriage, Duncan refused to speak to his parents as his mother wept into a handkerchief.

Lizzy's Bitterness

Charlotte had stopped crying and rose to her feet to confront her sister. 'Why?'

Lizzy stared into the tear filled blue eyes of her pretty sister and finally snapped. 'You always had everything, I had nothing but misery, drudgery and insults! I was sick and tired of living in your shadow and copping every day their corrosive abuse! When Duncan offered me the opportunity of getting rid of all of you, I jumped at the chance. I had nothing against Caleb and Tony but it was a small price to pay if we all got what we wanted. Freedom! I could've been Lady Elizabeth, Countess of Stirling instead of poor unwanted Lizzy!'

A single tear fell down Charlotte's cheek. 'I'm sorry Lizzy, I failed to get you out of that house. I should've tried harder.'

Lizzy's top lip curled. 'Should have but you didn't!' She didn't resist as Bell placed his hand under her elbow and led her towards the hallway.

Unable to deny the accusation, the Earl silently took his weeping wife into his arms to try to comfort her and guided her faltering steps up to her bedroom.

Reality For Patrick

Pausing in front of Tony, Patrick held out his hand towards her. She tightened her hold on her brother's hand and instinctively took a step backwards. Feeling a solid presence behind her and an arm circling her waist, Tony glanced up quickly to find Caleb supportively behind her.

'Ah sweet coz, no hard feelings beautiful girl. There were two things I wanted most in this world, you and the title. We could have been very good together my dear but...' Patrick elegantly shrugged his shoulders.

'But I insisted Papa remarry to produce a direct heir and I fell in love with someone other than you.' Tony finished for him.

Patrick's eyes closed to narrow slits as he purred, 'Yes, I had been patiently waiting for you to grow out of your tomboy habits before I approached you about marriage. It's almost as if Uncle Julius knew and deliberately re-introduced Delacourt to you to put a spoke in my wheels.'

'Of course he did!' The voice behind Tony and Caleb made her jump and they turned to where Frederick Sinclair was unashamedly eavesdropping.

'Julius was prepared to let Tony live out her days dressed as a man and never marry, rather than see her married to you Patrick.' The financial wizard drawled.

Tony cast a saucy look up at her new husband. 'No one said that was an option!'

Chuckling, Caleb tightened his arms around Tony's waist. 'Having second thoughts my elfling?'

'None whatsoever!' Tony turned in his arms and reached up with her free hand to bring Caleb's head down to kiss him.

'What a revolting display,' sighed Patrick with considerable pain in his voice. 'In front of your baby brother too!'

Aidan looked up as Caleb and Tony continued to kiss and cast a look of scorn back at Patrick. 'They're only kissing! They're allowed to do that now. And more than that! You're not welcome here anymore so go away now!' Turning his back Aidan missed Patrick's shocked expression at having been dismissed by a five year old.

Breaking off the kiss, Tony leant her head upon her husband's shoulder. 'Good bye Patrick, I don't regret persuading Papa remarry to produce Aidan. You would have made an unconvincing Earl.' Following Aidan's example, Tony turned her back on Patrick and with Caleb and Aidan by her side, she walked away.

We Had No Idea!

As the morning room began to empty, a shell shocked Reverend Gray and his wife Heather still sat immobile in their chairs. As Heather was trying to control her sobs, they looked more than a little lost, a little confused and more than a little mortified that this was actually the work of their own flesh and blood. With the suspects removed from the room, Aidan felt confident that he was now safe but as he released Tony's hand he did, though, keep a firm grip upon Caleb's hand as they followed Tony when she stepped towards the traumatised Grays. Heather blew her nose and tried to pull herself together as she and Matthew rose to their feet.

'Lady Tony, I can't begin to tell you how sorry we are about what our son has done.' Heather swallowed hard on the choking lump in her throat that made it impossible for her to even say Duncan's name. With an understanding smile, Tony held open her arms and with a sob Heather fell into her embrace.

'This is all my fault, I should have made Duncan aware of my presence the moment I stepped into the school room.' Tony ran a soothing hand along Heather's back as she cried.

'Nonsense!' Reverend Matthew Gray had finally managed to unhinge his locked jaw.

'My dear child, you may have avoided the adventure across France but consider what would've happened if his plan had actually succeeded? It wouldn't just be the loss of six lives. Duncan was planning a full scale revolution. Thousands…

millions could have died! Duncan's plan could have ignited not just a war between two nations but spread across the continent. We could have ended up with a global war!'

Caleb laid his free hand upon the Reverend's shoulder as he shook in rage. 'As angry, ashamed and hurt Duncan has made you, it is imperative that you learn why he felt this was necessary.'

'We cannot condone or support what he had planned.' The Reverend was appalled at the notion of starting a war.

Caleb shook his head, 'I know but it may have been logical in his mind.'

Drawing away from Tony, Heather wiped her handkerchief across her face and blew her nose again. 'Will... will they go to prison?' Her voice broke on a hiccup.

Shaking his head, Frederick Sinclair linked his wife's arm through his. 'I'm sorry Mrs Gray but Duncan has committed high treason and the sentence for that is death. Lizzy will face charges of murder and attempted murders and will face a similar sentence. I'm not certain about Patrick, he is complicit with the other two's actions but he may only get a prison sentence.'

Having been standing unseen in the corner of the room, Clive Dunn, the Earl's lawyer, cleared his throat. 'A clever lawyer may be able to prove provocation in the case of how Mrs Henry treated her daughter but there'll be no way to explain away the attempt to murder Lady Antonia, Lord Caleb or Lord Aidan.'

Frederick Sinclair glanced across to the lawyer. 'Get them a good lawyer Dunn. Obviously you can't represent them but they need a fair trial.'

'Of course Mr Sinclair,' the lawyer didn't even bat an eye lid at the financial wizard's request.

Heather, though, had a practical problem. 'We can't afford even a half decent lawyer Mr Sinclair. We were only able to send Duncan to university due to the generosity of Earl Stirling.

Matthew can't ask the Earl to pay for Duncan's legal fees when he was responsible for the attempt upon the Earl's children.'

Frederick nodded. 'I'll foot the bill.'

Heather stared at him open mouthed and speechless. Matthew managed to find his tongue.

'Why? Tony is your granddaughter! Why would you help the criminals who tried to kill her?'

'Because it is the right thing to do.' An enigmatic smile appeared on the financial genius' face. 'Oh I don't expect any court in this land will see them get off! They will hang for their crimes but after a fair and well represented trial. There will be no appeals due to incompetence on the part of their lawyer. Besides,' Frederick's smile softened as did his voice. 'When Julius is less angry, he will understand. I haven't forgotten what you both have done for this family.'

'Your support and comfort every time our Grace lost child after child. How you surrounded Julius and Tony with love and compassion when Grace and baby Michael were both taken from us. We're family Reverend, and that means accepting the good and the bad that comes along with being a family.' Pressing his lips against Tony's cheek, Frederick added, 'we'll just go and see how Lady Margarette is doing. Three shocks in one day may be a bit much for her.'

Squeezing the fingers that briefly touched hers, Tony smiled. 'Thank you Grandpapa, for everything.'

Preston arranged for the Earl's own carriage to take Matthew and Heather Gray home before he and Mrs Preston headed downstairs to reveal the truth to all the servants. Isabella went upstairs with Louise to freshen up before dinner. Phillippe strode out to stand down the Moreau brothers, once the criminals and the Bow Street Runners escort were safely on the road to London.

The lawyer, Clive Dunn slipped out of the morning room to commandeer the Earl's study to write up the spectacular revelations they had just witnessed. As shocking as the news of the newlyweds and their brother's death had been, Doctor Masters knew that the revelation of the identity of the guilty parties and the news that the intended victims weren't in fact dead would be just as shocking. So he had already headed, medical bag in hand, upstairs to assess and administer medical aid where-ever it was needed.

Is It Really Over Now?

So that left in the room with Tony, Caleb and Aidan; François, Andre, Rosemary, William and Mary. Even though they had been privy to the ruse, the two women hugged Tony in relief that it was finally over.

'Oh my Lady, I don't ever want to go through anything like the past fortnight ever again!' Mary angrily brushed away a tear that fell down her face.

Rosemary giggled. 'I couldn't believe the look on everyone's faces when the three of you appeared in the doorway.'

Chuckling as he sat on the edge of the table that had recently been used by Bell, Andre added, 'I won't ever forget the look on everyone's faces when first Caleb kissed Geoff and then he let him kiss his bride. That was priceless!'

Grinning boyishly, Caleb slid his arm around Tony's waist. 'I didn't think I could go through with it when Phillippe told us that Geoff needed some physical contact to determine his true feelings towards me. If he had proved to be guilty, I certainly wouldn't have done it. I don't think Geoff or I will be kissing any other men any time soon.'

From where he stood leaning against the wall beside the door, François laughed mischievously. 'I think I could make you change your minds about that!'

Tony shook her head. 'That is not fair François, you're different. No man or woman could resist you.'

Andre's eyebrows rose in interest. 'Meaning what Tony? Have you succumbed to the young god's beauty?'

Blushing, Tony knew that Caleb cast a startled look down at her. 'No, I have my own god-like husband but to be kissed by François would be like the touch of an angel. Like Theodore, François' beauty seems to defy belief that anyone could look like that and still be human.' As Tony broke off breathless, Caleb tried to keep any feelings of jealousy out of his voice.

'I'm starting to feel very insecure elfling.' Turning into her husband's arms, Tony placed her hands on either side of Caleb's face.

'I'll show you later that you're the only man I will ever want!' She kissed him lightly but her eyes promised him so much more in their very near future.

Taking Rosemary's hand into his own, Andre said, 'So what happens now? Is this happily ever after or is it just that the next chapter is waiting to be written?'

'I suppose you and Rosemary will head back to Paris with her brothers and Madame Martin to plan for your own wedding.' At Tony's words, Rosemary blushed prettily.

'Louise and I will be staying here at the Manor,' François added, 'there's some legal work to take care of before we head over to Ireland so that I can meet my future bride.'

Surprise was written over Andre's face. 'Phillippe would never allow you to be forced into an arranged marriage.'

Smiling, François shook his head. 'I get to choose the cousin I wish to marry. It's even possible that I might fall in love, if not,' the young god's eyes met those of Theodore Moreau, who stood just outside the room and they both smiled. 'Well there are always other… distractions.' François finally added, 'Excuse me.' He headed out to join the other celestial being.

'Lord Caleb,' Mary started hesitantly, 'can you promise me that this is not going to become the normal way of life now that you're married?'

'Getting cold feet Mary?' Caleb's eyes twinkled. 'You've known Tony since she was a child, did she ever do anything that was normal?'

'Hey!' Tony protested but couldn't honestly deny the charge, especially when Mary agreed with Caleb.

'No, my Lord. William and I have a request,' Mary paused as she struggled to get the right words out.

'The other options are still available if you don't want to come to Delacourt Hall.' Caleb said, understanding their reservations.

'Oh no, my Lord, we're coming with you but we would like to be married, spend a little time with our families then go to Delacourt Hall before you and Lady Tony move there permanently.'

'Of course but may I ask why move into the Hall before us?' Caleb asked.

'We want to acclimatise ourselves to how your servants do things. It will be nicer for you to have everything running smoothly when you can finally leave Lord Aidan.' Mary admitted.

Releasing her new husband, Tony hugged her loyal and staunch Maid. 'You are one in a million Mary! Thank you!'

'Now, now, my Lady, enough of that! Do you wish to change before dinner?' Mary disengaged herself from her young employer.

'No, thank you but I think we should go down to the servants' domain to support Preston's assurances that we are in fact not ghosts.' Tony cast up a questioning glance at Caleb to make certain that this was appropriate.

'An excellent idea,' Caleb's smile caused a flutter of excitement in Tony's stomach.

'It's a pity we don't have a little longer before we need to assemble for dinner.' Tony tenderly caressed her hand down Caleb' cheek. His sudden indrawn breath meant he knew exactly what his bride was hinting. It seemed as though everyone else in the room understood as well. Including Aidan.

'If you want to be alone for a while tonight,' the little Lord was trying to be brave about being separated from his sister and new brother. 'Can I sleep in my own room with Mary and William to protect me?'

Tony crouched down so that she was eye level with her brother. 'We don't want to do anything that will make you frightened.'

'But I'll be able to come back to you once you've finished being married naughty, won't I?'

'Yes of course,' his sister promised.

'That's all right then.' The tension left Aidan, knowing that any separation would be temporary, for now.

Watching as the siblings hugged, Caleb felt pleasure and yet pain. *As much as I want, need to finally be one with my bride, I will somehow find the strength to suppress my desires if it means causing even a minute of fear in my new little brother.* Holding out his hand to Aidan, Caleb said, 'Would you like to be carried Little Bear?'

As Tony straightened upright again, Aidan glanced searchingly up at Caleb. 'Are we in any more danger?'

'No, I think we're safe enough now.' Caleb could see something revolving around the young boy's brain.

'Then I can walk. I'm not a baby, big brother.'

'No, you're not a baby, Little Bear.' *There is so much tenderness in Caleb's voice that I find myself even more in love with my husband but I'll refrain from tearing his clothes off here and now. Something significant is enacting between the new brothers,* mused Tony.

'How about a piggy back then? That's not for babies is it?' asked Caleb.

Aidan's eyes lit up at the offer but some sudden thought brought a frown to his brow and his hands stopped half way in reaching out to Caleb.

'Caleb, I saw your chest when we were changing. That bruising… I… I don't want to do any further damage to your heart.' The young Lord's admission nearly tore Andre's heart out of his chest but he bit his bottom lip as Caleb crouched down in front of Aidan.

'You can't damage my heart Little Bear,' Caleb took Aidan's hand and laid it against his steady heartbeat. 'It's too full of love for you and Tony that nothing but losing either of you could hurt me now.'

Aidan threw himself whole heartedly into Caleb's arms, almost knocking him flat on his back. In delight, Andre clapped his hand before hugging Rosemary to him.

'I am so going to write your story mes enfants! All of it! Even if it can never be published! This story must be told!'

Sympathetically, Tony patted the excited Author on the back as William assisted Caleb to his feet and swung Aidan round onto his back.

'Yes you must write of our adventures,' agreed Aidan, his arms around Caleb's neck and his legs wrapped around his brother's waist. 'I want to be able to read about it when I'm old enough to understand what really happened.' Aidan paused as Tony and Caleb cast guilty but tender looks at each other.

'But Tony, there is one thing that you really must remember.' Aidan's eyes opened wider as he glanced innocently at his sister.

'What is that Little Bear?' *I don't think I could ever forget anything about what had occurred the past twelve days.*

'When you and Caleb are naughty, you must remember to lock the door.'

Bursting out into laughter, Andre fell off the table as Tony and Caleb smiled at each other.

'Most definitely!' Tony agreed, linking her arm through her husband's and they left behind them an adventure they would never forget. Or would want to.

ABOUT THE AUTHOR

Anne-Marie Price was born and raised in Perth, Western Australia. She lives with her parents Margaret and Laurence and has two cats, Mickey and Jackson.

She has been a member of the Society of Women Writers WA since 2009 and has been their secretary since 2011.

Anne-Marie has had articles and flash fiction stories published in the SWW In Print Magazine as well as The Readers World Magazine.

In 1997, she obtained a Degree– Library And Information Studies, in 1998 a Diploma of Comprehensive Writing and in 2009 a Cert IV Training and Assessment to assist her ability to teach others the craft of writing.

Writing is in the blood of the Price family with Anne-Marie being the fourth generation of writers. Anne-Marie has been writing fiction since the age of ten and still uses pen and paper as a preference for a first draft.

Also By This Author

Hostage Of Diplomacy
2015
Contemporary Romance

The Search For The King James Bible
2015
Supernatural Romance

Stirling Trilogy
2016
Historical Romance